THE PULL

Other novels by Bobby Jack Nelson:

The Last Station
Brothers

THE PULL

BOBBY JACK NELSON

ST. MARTIN'S PRESS · NEW YORK

Design by Paolo Pepe

Library of Congress Cataloging in Publication Data
Nelson, Bobby Jack.
   The Pull.
   I. Title.
PS3564.E45B85   1986   813'.54   85-25090
ISBN 0-312-65572-X

First Edition

10 9 8 7 6 5 4 3 2 1

2274233

For Toben,
for his special gifts to me.

ACKNOWLEDGMENTS

Several people have been important in the realization of this book. I want to thank in particular my agent, Joan Brandt; my editor, Brian DeFiore; and that exquisite artist in my life, Pat Lincoln.

I am the shadow that follows the child.
I am the hunger of a young wolf.
I am the roaring of the rain.
I am the whole dream of these things.
You see, I am alive, I am alive.

—N. Scott Momaday

THE PULL

1

Our camp was in the trees again, in a clearing, and we'd just finished the garden.

Sailor was sharpening his ax, and I was imagining those seeds I'd planted beginning to soften and change. I was seeing them beneath the earth absorbing a dark nourishment through their skins until they were bloated and splitting, and I was envisioning their tiny shoots uncoiling and straightening. Their pushing upward then would be relentless until they broke through the crust and breathed in the open air, and I was breathing with them. . . .

But the air had changed. It was thinner somehow and I began to sense a curious tightening in the ground. In the west the clouds were rising and turning black. A wind was starting a distant turmoil in the trees. Suddenly the sky was being shoved to one side and I could feel the vacuum of the storm's approach pulling my face.

I crawled under the wagon for cover and in the next instant the thing stopped. There was a halt, an interlude of sorts, and a calmness descended. A stillness spread itself through the trees and for a while the air was nearly dead. The early dark was wide and quiet.

I felt a smoothness inside, a kind of goodness, and I never knew when the rain began. It was simply there and softly falling.

At the same time a crack of light appeared, a long slow strip of white, and the sky was broken apart and ripped in half. An explosion of thunder shattered the clouds and the weight of the storm crashed down. The winds came whipping the rain. Bolts of lightning struck the ground and rolled into bursting balls. Pockets of air were wafting about, electrified and singing, and the rain was left shimmering.

The wagon protected me but Sailor was still in the clearing. He was staying out in it, raising his arms up to it and calling it down. "Yeeow! C'mon! Let 'er rip! Pour 'er down!"

"You're crazy!" I shouted. "You're gonna get struck!" But he didn't care. He was laughing.

Judy and Mawd were silhouetted in flashes at their tethers and I could see their eyes rolling. They were up on their hind legs in a frantic dance to run and their dark coats were streaming, gleaming wet.

The gully below was rushing its banks and rivulets down the slope were widening into chutes, flooding our garden. The rows I'd planted were disappearing in a tide of foam and mud.

Sailor's face came down into mine. "Hey, kid, whatcha scared of?" A dripping, bristly face with shining eyes. "Hey, c'mon," he grinned, "have some fun."

The wet air suddenly exploded in our faces, and thunder shook the ground.

When I looked again, Sailor was gone and there were loose lines dangling in the trees. There was a blank spot where Judy and Mawd had been and the sound of their hooves was splashing away in the storm.

Sailor had started after them and stopped. He was in the clearing and limbs all around were shuddering in the flickering night. Rain was whipping his clothes, and he was illuminated by lightning. It appeared to break against him and envelop him. His battered face was a part of the violence and he was calling me. "C'mon, ya want 'em to run over a cliff and break a leg? We gotta go after 'em!"

I couldn't move. If I went out there, I'd get struck for sure. A bolt would pick me off. Or one of those sizzling balls would bounce on me and burn me to death.

"C'mon!" he yelled.

"I can't—you go on!"

But he didn't move. He was going to wait me out.

"I'll get struck, Sailor, dammit, I will. I'll get killed out there!"

"What about them? You don't care, do you?"

All at once the whole of the sky blossomed. A great flash exposed the windy treetops, the swimming ground, and we were only glittering bits in the whorl.

"Sailor, I can't!"

"Then you don't care, you don't care about Judy and Mawd!"

I saw them in my mind looking at me, two dumb creatures with sad eyes, with their stupid lower lips hanging and their ears drooped in disappointment—but with feelings still, real feelings.

That did it.

I left the wagon and ran to Sailor. "All right, you wait, I'm gonna get struck, you'll see!" I felt wild-eyed.

"Hell, it's only a storm." He laughed. "C'mon, you're gonna live forever." He slapped my shoulder and started at a trot down the logging trail that was now a twisting slough.

It was all I could do to keep up. The ground was slush and the downpour was blinding. I was bogging to my shins in mud. And snakes too, I figured, were writhing in that mess. I could feel them slithering around my ankles. I saw dead arms reaching from the trees.

Sailor was hey-ho-ing for Judy and Mawd but the storm was too loud and the wind was howling. Lightning revealed us sopping, our bodies contorted, our shirts plastered to our ribs. The rain was beating our faces and I felt a chill. The thought of pneumonia seized my brain and I saw myself wracked with fever and dying. My teeth started chattering.

Sailor stopped. "Now what's the matter?"

"I think I'm sick."

"What're you talking about?"

"I am. I'm catching pneumonia."

"It's not even cold."

"Just the same."

"C'mon—"

"You don't care if I die, or what."

4

"Hey, what's got into you?"

"You don't." I felt a craziness building. "You don't give a damn what happens to me."

"Now how can you say that?" He said that with a straight face, in all innocence.

"How can I say that!" I heard myself shouting in a shrill voice. "I'll tell you how, because you got me nearly stabbed to death and you didn't care! That man pulled that knife and you had me in the middle, right in between, and he didn't miss my neck that far!" I measured the miss with my thumb and finger in his face.

"Aw, c'mon, Bud—"

"Not that far! I could've been dead now!" My nose was running and I was sniveling.

"But that was years ago, Bud. You were just a kid."

His voice sounded reasonable and I felt abruptly stopped. He was right too. It had been years. But it seemed like yesterday, that man and Sailor drunk in the alley, and me in between, and that big knife was arching the round lamplight.

"Just the same," I said, "you don't care."

He patted my head and splattered the rain in my hair. "C'mon, we'll find Judy and Mawd and then go back and get dry. You'll feel better."

He squeezed my shoulder. "You look thataway, I'll look over here." He shoved me off to the left.

It was immediately darker and I was smaller. The storm had me isolated in that moment and rushed in for the kill. It blew me down and tried to fasten me with limbs. The mud rose to suck me under. All I could think was to save myself. Sailor had vanished and left me alone and I was nowhere.

I think I went a little crazy. I was running to save myself and just then a bright streak came down. I was lifted and suspended. There was instant silence. A tree in front of me was slowly parting. I remember thinking people don't live like this. A beautiful sliver of light was splitting the tree in half and it was shining. Real people live in houses and stay dry, I thought. I heard an explosion somewhere. A brilliant glow was all around, pulsing, spurting outward. . . .

They said he'd come from the sea. He'd swooped me up and lifted me above his head and I was looking down at the red and blue tattoos on his arms. "So you're the kid? You grown so I wouldn't have known." He hefted me. "Who're you?" I said. His eyes widened. "Who'm I?" He hefted me higher. "Who'm I, the kid says!" He was laughing, and I was afraid he was going to throw me away.

When I came to, the storm had passed but long limbs of lightning still cracked the sky in the distance. I felt I was waking inside a great eggshell that was faintly breaking above me.

The tree nearby was split and smoking and Sailor was squatted beside me. He was picking something off my chest as if idly passing the time.

I pushed his hand away. "I told you," I said, and my voice surprised me, that I had one. "I told you I'd get struck, and I did."

"Had a close one, didn't ya?" He grinned meanly.

"You didn't believe me."

"Well, you're all right, you're not dead."

I felt for my face and it didn't seem to be there. My eyelashes were gone. There was only a powdery feel where my eyebrows had been and my forehead had turned to dust. There was no feeling at my nose or mouth.

"Oh, lord," I said, "I don't have a face anymore."

"Yeh, sometimes it's a victory just to wake up alive." Sailor stood up. "Well, you just gonna lay there or what?"

"I think I'm hurt."

"Naw, stunned maybe. You can walk around and shake it off."

"But I can't feel anything."

"All right, if you want me to, I can go ahead and bury you. I can dig a hole right here and put you down in it and shovel the dirt down over you, if you want that."

It would be mud he'd have to pack down and I imagined the gloppy shovelfuls plopping down on me.

"C'mon," he said, and he helped me to my feet. My whole body felt lame and willowy, and I was dizzy.

I looked around. "Judy and Mawd?"

"Gone."

"And the garden?"

"That too."

"And my face's gone."

"No, you didn't get that lucky, not quite."

I took a deep breath. "I was nearly killed, wasn't I?"

"Oh, maybe. Everybody has a close one now and then."

I hobbled along and thought about that. Everybody. What did everybody have to do with me? Everybody was somebody else, not me. "I don't care," I said. "I'm not everybody. I'm me."

"Yeh." He blew one side of his nose to the wind. "That's what everybody says."

.   .   .

The next morning Judy and Mawd were still gone. "We'll look for 'em later," Sailor said. "Maybe tomorrow, when you're feeling better." He kept his eyes diverted when he said that. It might have seemed a kindness.

But I was grateful. I was still weak and needed the rest. My face was also a bother. It was tender and blistered so smoothly I couldn't tell if I had any features left. It felt so blank I imagined I was seeing though a mask, or that it must look like a snake's face. I greased it with lard to keep it from scaling and sat as still as I could. The grease would attract gnats, but after the storm there were no gnats and I was able to sit in peace.

I tried not to notice the ruined place where my garden had been. Too many green dreams would still be there, and with me, if I didn't watch it, some dreams had a way of lingering longer than they should.

I concentrated instead on Sailor felling another tree, and Sailor with an ax was a fine show. His swing was long and powerful. At the same time he had a rhythm that was graceful and easy. His stance was wide and every arch he swung in the air was a perfect curve. His arms and back seemed one with the ax and he never missed a mark. He sliced into the tree so cleanly and smoothly there was no hurt. The wood appeared eager to yield and the tree seemed to want it, all those strokes going into it, the deeper and harder the better. It was a fascinating thing to watch.

A tree to Sailor, I think, was a singular thing, a

kind of individual. He knew them all so well. He'd approach each with a certain respect and say a few words and touch at them. He liked to put his hands on them. Then he'd go on and chop them down.

He never used a saw, he said, because there was no truth in that, and I got to where I loved the smell of fresh clean wood, especially in the early morning.

Since then years have passed and a lot of my feelings have been a long time withdrawn from play, but the woods remain. And so does the ax.

I watched Sailor fell the tree and since I was allowed the time to revive, I didn't have to strip the branches, and since we didn't have our mules to pull the timber out to the road for loading, Sailor let it lay and went on to mark the hardwoods we'd be cutting later.

I sat at our tent in the clearing. And left alone, I began to miss those mules, Judy and Mawd. Their hairs still stuck from the tree they liked to rub and their smells were still somehow strong and alive in the air. Pods remained where they had strolled and lazied about, and there was that dip where they liked to roll their bodies and dust their backs, a mud patch now, but I saw it dry as before, and I kept feeling a white powdery nuzzle at my palm.

I became sentimental. We'd lived as a family. We'd worked as partners. I knew their moods and they knew mine. Now their harnesses were empty and misshapen without them and the wagon tongue looked forlorn straight to the ground. I got a lump in my throat and felt stupid.

From time to time I whistled and waited for some snort or blowing in reply, or that special squeak in the sound of their hooves, but nothing came back. As the day passed I began to worry the bald ledges that had once been my eyebrows.

In another month, I remembered, I was going to have a birthday. I was going to be fourteen.

By nightfall, when Judy and Mawd were still gone, I tried to convince myself it was best, and I began to feel an odd sense of relief. It would be better, actually, without them. We wouldn't be so tied down then. We wouldn't always have to be tending them, seeing that they were forever watered and fed. Without them, we could be free of their inferior type reputation too. Besides, nobody worked with mules anymore. We could get a truck like everybody else and people would quit looking at us like we were different. Our lives could change. We could move into a town where there were things to do and we could belong somewhere.

But we'd been together so long, Judy and Mawd and me, we knew each other so well, there was that attachment. A kind of personal relationship that you don't end just like that.

That night I was restless in my sleep with wild and contrary dreams.

The next morning we started looking. The creek had risen too high to cross in places and the valley had flooded, but we walked the hills on both sides of the logging road and went where we could as far as the canyon. We kept whistling and calling out, "Hey, Mawdy, Jude! Hey, Judymawd!"

Sailor also kept his eye out for any gold the rains might have flushed. When he saw a likely-looking off-colored rock, he'd pick it up and bite at it. All together, I suppose, he bit at about twenty rocks, and they all turned out failures, not in the least graced with fortune.

He never found gold, and we never found a trace of our mules either.

I figured the search had been for nothing. But Sailor said, "No, hun-uh, not for nothing. For something. We were looking, weren't we?"

"And found nothing."

"But we found what was out there."

"Which was nothing."

"Which we wouldn't've found if we hadn't looked. So that makes it something."

Something was nothing, and nothing was something. That's the way he always talked, and I let it drop. It was so senseless it wasn't even funny.

Back at camp I was roasting the rabbit over the fire. Sailor had killed it with a stick—he could hit so quick—and he'd skinned it in a manner I couldn't, slitting it around the throat and down the stomach and then stomping on its head to peel the fur. That was his method, and he could skin any small animal that way in a flash, but I could never get used to the feel of their tiny skulls under my heel.

"I hate to give it up," he said. He had another odd rock in his hand, turning it over. "But I guess they're lost. Might as well face it."

The rabbit was turning golden brown and making me hungry. The fat was dripping and causing the flames to sputter.

"If they were coming back," Sailor said, "they would've already. I guess they got too far, though, got lost." He weighed his rock thoughtfully. "Or maybe somebody picked 'em off."

I felt a chill on my neck. "The river rats," I said. A colony of those type people were close by, we knew. We'd caught glimpses of them through the trees a couple of times.

"Yeh, maybe."

"What if it was them?" I said.

He looked at me. "You wanna go back in there and ask 'em?"

He knew my answer to that. A man could walk into a nest of those river rats and never be seen again.

I concentrated on the rabbit. Those river rats were a subhuman race apart. They lived back in the woods along the river like a colony of rodents, inbreeding and duplicating themselves until they all had the same sightless cast to their faces and the same mouths full of deranged teeth. They lived with lice in their hair and tapeworms in their bowels.

"I guess we go into town tomorrow," Sailor said. "We'll go by the auction and get us a couple more."

"A couple more what?"

"Work animals, what else?"

"Work animals," I repeated. The words had such a foreign sound. "Work animals don't have names," I said. "Judy and Mawd had names."

"Well, Judy and Mawd are gone."

"You weren't trying to find 'em anyway. You were just looking for gold, that's all you wanted to find."

"I might strike it someday too."

"You're never gonna strike it."

"Who sez?"

"You never have."

For a peculiar instant he looked hurt. Then his eyes changed and he grinned. "Yeh, I have too."

"When?"

"Before you were born. I saw a vein once as wide as that creek, pure gold you didn't even have to smelt. I saw it as clear as day shining up out of the water, big chunks—"

"In your head! That's the only place you've ever seen it, Sailor, in your crazy head!"

"But I've seen it."

"But not for real, you've never seen it for real!" I was almost screaming.

"Hey, calm down." He leaned back. "What's got into you?"

"Nothing." I looked away and started picking at my face. The blistered parts felt like they were beginning to peel.

Sailor looked away also and stared into the night and we had another one of our silences.

We were always living in trees somewhere, in a tent or shack, away from people. I didn't know why he'd taken me. I had been living in a house with Murph and Mattie, and I had a dog with brown-and-white spots. I had a bed to sleep in and Mattie made fried apple pies for me. We had a garden and my name was Bobby, but Sailor took me away and started calling me Bud. He'd been at sea, they said. He'd come from the sea, and that's why he had tattoos, but I didn't kow why he took me away. He said he was my father, but I'd been happy—even if I couldn't remember everything, I was so young, I remember that. Mattie left the lamp on beside my bed so I wouldn't be afraid of the dark. . . .

Sailor stood up and pitched his rock into the fire. "Yeh, we'll go into town tomorrow and stop by the auction."

"We're not going to find another team as good as Judy and Mawd," I said.

"No, probably not."

"They pulled everything we asked them to."

"That's right, they did."

"They pulled perfect together, even across the draws."

"Well, we'll see what we can come up with."

"Why don't we just get a truck?"

I could have stabbed him, from the way he suddenly tensed. I'd said the wrong thing and I knew it, but I couldn't help it. A truck was a chance.

"I told you"—he clenched his teeth—"don't bring that up again. We ain't gonna be *mechanized*." He made it sound dirty.

I tried to smooth it over. "Well, maybe Judy and Mawd'll come back yet."

He shook his head. "It's been two days. We could wait forever—No, we'll just go into town tomorrow and get us a couple more."

I could tell he wanted to go into town for other reasons too. He was working his mouth that certain way.

When he caught me looking, knowing, he turned his back and moved out of sight.

I sat there absently and cooked the rabbit until it was a charcoal lump.

. . .

He'd told me about my mother once. "She was Injun," he said. I remember reacting, feeling strange. "It's all right," he said. "She was Kiowa."

"Kiowa," I repeated. The word was a wonderful sound in my mouth. It echoed in my head. "What was she like?"

"She was pretty, very pretty—" He stopped. "That's enough."

I imagined her eyes dark and shiny, her hair black and braided. She'd have turquoise around her neck and hold her head high, and she'd be proud. I saw her riding a spotted pony through the clouds.

"You can stand it," he said. "It'll make you tougher."

So I learned, when you start with an ax, your hand gets blisters, and when you keep chopping, the blisters break, the skin peels back, and the next layer is raw. Before long your hands start bleeding and you can feel them wearing through. By the end of the day you know you're damaged. Your fingers have curled into claws and the pain has settled in to last the night.

The next day you have to make yourself go, the handle's so hard to touch. Your eyes water when you take it up, and you don't want it to slip on the raw places, so you grip it tight and bear the clinch up in your arms up to your shoulders. When you start swinging again, you know your hands are being worn to the bone. You get a good picture of it in your mind.

But you bear it and your hands don't wear away. Something else happens. At the last moment the skin starts building back. The hands fight back and start taking care of themselves. They lay on calluses and refuse to give in. And then they're tough with layers of calluses and nothing hurts them.

"And you're the same," Sailor said. "Call it conflict, struggle, whatever. Bear with it, stand it awhile, you end up stronger."

That's what he'd tell me and it sounded good. I'd seen it work with my hands, and I wanted to believe it, but the rest of me, I figured, was something else.

• • •

It was ten miles into town, about a three-hour walk.
Before long, Sailor was out ahead with his long strides
and I was falling behind.

"Hey, wait up," I called.

"C'mon." He wasn't stopping.

"I can't keep up."

"You better."

But I can't, I thought, I can't ever keep up.

Then he stopped for a leak and I caught up. It always took him a long time to relieve himself. Standing
with one hand braced against a tree, leaning forward,
there'd be a kind of pained expression on his face and
he'd grunt and empty in dribbles. I figured something
was wrong but he never said what it was and I didn't
ask. You get sick, that's your own business. I think that
was more or less the rule between us.

About halfway to town we also stopped for a rest. And
in that particular spot in the woods it was nice. Little
flowers were blooming and vines were nearly crawling,
they were growing so fast. Above where I sat, a redbird
perched a limb. I knew if I looked around, I'd see more
too. Toads in the mud and guineas in the bush, and
spiders in chilling and wonderful shapes. Life searching the ground furtively and flying the air. Squirrels
and chipmunks and foxes. Scissortails chasing the
sparrows. Brown moccasins sunning themselves on the
creek bank. Green turtles on a drifting log. A log also
looking solid and whole but crumbling to the touch.
The skeleton of some carcass eaten by maggots. The
rotting root and dead pond and the small brittle thing
caught in a web. The hull and husk of this and that,

16

and off in the distance, if you listened hard, the faint cry of something hurt or dying.

You could look and see it all, the living and the dying, and in the woods it never stops.

Except, after a while, without people, it gets lonely. But that's something you learn to live with, Sailor said, and you let it have its uses. You figure loneliness is a part of life. It's as old as creation, perhaps a condition of creation itself, and you get used to it. You handle it and not let it make you feel sorry. So Sailor said.

He was staring vacantly at his hands while we sat resting. It was a strange thing he'd started doing more often lately and I couldn't figure it.

I realize now, of course, he'd come to that point in his life where he was no longer allowed to see further ahead than behind, and he'd come to it at the wrong time, in the spring of the year when the rest of the world was blooming and renewing itself, and he wasn't. But I didn't know that then.

He finally took a breath and raised his eyes.

"What?" I said.

"I dunno," he said. "I was just thinking, you go out and cut down trees and you think that's it. But the first thing you know, you look around and they've grown back right behind you."

"Not right away."

"Right away or in twenty years, what's the difference? It's all the same. You cut a track and it grows back like you'd never been there. You think you've made a dent, but you haven't. You can't even tell where you've been."

"Maybe we oughta quit cutting trees."

He slapped at something in front of his face. "And then what?"

"Maybe we could do something else." An idiot hope leaped in my chest. "Maybe we could get a job in town, at the sawmill or someplace." We could live in a house with a refrigerator and watch television. We could have people next door.

He gave me a look. "And punch a time clock and kiss ass—you'd be better off in prison."

"It wouldn't be like that."

"What do you know? You've been living free your whole life. You try one of them fine jobs in town, eight to five, working for somebody else every minute, you'll find out. You don't know how lucky you are, that's your problem."

"I just thought we could try it."

"I've already tried it. No, thank you."

"But you were thinking, you know, like what's the use cutting trees."

"I was talking about something else. Now forget it. We're doing what we want to." He stood up abruptly and started on.

I called after him, "You say we're doing what we want to, but you never asked me!"

"That's right," he answered without looking back. "I don't have to." He was a purpose all his own.

For the first time it went all over me. He was walking away and I grabbed a rock to hurl at the back of his skull. I wanted to bash his brains out and kill him and be finished with him. I'd be free then, free of all my troubles wrapped in one. His back was to me, and he wouldn't see it coming, and I drew back to let go.

But I couldn't do it. I was too shaky and he was like solid oak, like an ox. Even if I made a direct hit, it wouldn't hurt him. The rock would bounce off, and he'd turn around and then no telling what he'd do. I'd seen him in fights and he was like a madman.

The rock dribbled out of my hand on its own, and I found myself once again following after him. I became the rear end of a little abbreviated single file, not exactly marching, but almost the same. It didn't take any brains.

But I was trying to think. I needed to make some plans and do something to get away. I was big enough and I had money of my own, nearly fifty dollars. It was in a pouch on a string around my neck and it was enough to go on. And that's what I'd do. I'd take off and go somewhere he couldn't find me. I'd make up a new name for myself and start a new life and be happy. I'd pretend to be somebody else, an experienced fry cook or maybe a carpenter.

The only thing was, right now, I had the problem with my face, or rather the problem of not having one. No eyebrows or anything. People would look at me and think I was a freak. So I'd have to do something about that first thing.

We reached the highway and walked on the left to face traffic. For the first time we were going into town without the team and wagon, and I was glad. Riding the wagon to town was something I'd grown to dread. It was all right in the country. It was natural there. But in town it turned us into outlandish sort of characters and a kind of spectacle. Everybody gawked at us so, and we'd poke along, and the cars would stack up behind us and honk.

So this was better. Without those damned mules, much better. Like suddenly being freed. I felt a new spring in my step and a lift in my spirits. Except for not having a car, we were going to town almost like normal human beings.

At the same time, without Judy and Mawd, something was missing. Down deep, where I kept things waiting, it wasn't all airy and light.

But we were going to town. And that was something.

In the middle of the one main street Sailor slapped my shoulder. "You're on your own. I'll see you tomorrow at the auction barn."

He was moving away, and I grabbed his sleeve. "What about tonight?"

"Get you a room at the Belvedere."

"And you're going to meet me tomorrow at the auction?"

"That's what I said, didn't I?"

"I know how you do, though."

"You worry like an old woman." He slapped my shoulder again and started off.

"At the auction," I yelled after him, "and you better be there too!" I don't know why I said that. If I could figure a way, I wasn't going to be there either.

Sailor was heading for Dominoes, for their back room, where they had drinks and played poker. And that's what he'd be doing, drinking and gambling, and I could see him, winning at first, with his bristly face shining, because he nearly always started out winning and happy, and then he'd keep drinking and get drunk and start losing. Every time. He'd have his fun and when there wasn't any more, he'd make his way to Pauline's cathouse on the edge of town and have himself a whore. Or he'd get in a fight or some mess and end up overnight in jail. Sometimes, when he couldn't pay his fine, he'd have to stay locked up a couple of days and I'd have to wait for him to get out.

In any town he could find himself a Dominoes and a place like Pauline's.

"You can't forget to live," he'd say.

"Some living," I'd say. "You lose all our money."

"Well, just remember, kid, there ain't no wealth but life."

And I'd think, yeah, sure, except we're always broke and scrounging. Where's the wealth in that kind of life?

I watched him go into Dominoes down the street and I knew I had the rest of the day and night to myself. And maybe the next day and night too.

. . .

Now, in a department store most people make the mistake of dawdling, and that's wrong. That causes suspicion. The best way is to walk in, don't look around, head straight for what you want, sneak it, and get out. If somebody sees you, they don't believe it. They think you must have a reason, you've been so open.

This department store had a stack of good caps on the front counter and it was so easy I almost hesitated. But I didn't. I walked in bareheaded and came out with a brown duckbill pulled down over my eyes.

Then, with at least the top part of my face covered, I headed for the drugstore.

It had been three months since I'd been in, but the same girl was still behind the old-fashioned fountain, and I was hoping she would be. Her name was Hominy. Or that was the name on the little plastic card pinned to her shirt. But since we'd never actually met, I'd never said two words to her.

This time, though, I was going to.

But first I stopped at the magazine rack to screw up the nerve and to look at her without being noticed.

She had changed. I pretended to thumb a magazine, a hot-rod thing. Her hair was shorter, and her eyes were distinctly different. They were larger and darker. They were made up, and her lips were redder. A bright red. Her mouth was somehow sadder and prettier than I'd remembered, and her breasts were larger. She looked older.

I felt disturbed. She was more mature. And that was it. In three months she had grown mature and left me behind. She had to be fifteen, maybe sixteen, and that was older than me. She looked experienced too, and I wasn't.

It was a blow, and I felt dejected. The magazine turned to a blur in my hands. She was beyond me. I was never going to get a girl.

Then suddenly I felt a surprising relief. If she was out of reach, there was no problem. If I couldn't win, I couldn't lose. I didn't have to worry about failing or acting a fool. Whatever I did wasn't going to make the least impression on her.

I sat at the counter in a jaunty mood. I could handle an ax. I could handle myself with a girl. When she came by, I ordered a Coke. I gave her a look and she pretended not to notice. Which was fine. What the hell. I'd give her a look if I wanted to. I took a straw to fiddle with and purposely pushed my cap back to reveal my face. What difference did it make? Anybody didn't like it, they could lump it. I was tougher than I looked. You swing an ax all your life you get pretty strong, especially in your arms and shoulders. A few wise guys had found that out. I'd surprised 'em. I didn't want to fight, but if I had to, I could take care of myself. And that's what you had to do in this life, take care of yourself. That's what I was going to start doing too. To hell with Sailor.

Hominy set a Coke in front of me, and I leaned forward with my face, but my rimless eyes didn't faze her. She wasn't one bit shocked.

She only said, "So what's your problem?"

"I was in an accident."

"You look like it."

"I was struck by lightning."

One corner of her pretty mouth went up. "Yeah? Tell me another one."

"I was."

"And you lived to tell about it."

"I was out in the storm about three nights ago and I was struck by a bolt, knocked me out like a light."

"You're kidding."

"My feet were wet. That makes a good conductor."

"You're kidding me." She wanted to believe me.

"No, honest, I'm telling the truth."

"It must've hurt."

"Yeah, but when I came to, I just got up and walked away."

"You were lucky."

"I know it. I could've been dead now."

She went down the counter to wait on someone else and I sat in a glow with my Coke. I'd talked with her easy and she'd acted impressed. I'd even impressed myself. Not just anybody can get struck by lightning and live to tell about it. Maybe I had a chance with her, after all. I could ask to meet her when she got off work and we could go have a hamburger at the drive-in and talk some more. If she had troubles, she could tell me and I'd listen. I'd be around and she could learn to depend on me. Maybe we could kiss.

"That it?" She was back to write my check.

"I better have another one." I gulped what was in front of me. "I'm kinda thirsty."

She scooped ice and started another Coke at the fountain. Her arm pulling the lever was lightly freckled. A beautiful arm. She rested her weight on one foot with her hip cocked and I could see the outline of her panties.

"My name's Bud," I said. But I wanted to be truthful, so I added, "Well, it's really Bobby, but that's what I'm called—Bud."

She gave me a slanting glance from behind the lever.

Now I lied. "We've met before."

"When was that?"

"When I was in before, about three months ago. Maybe you don't remember."

She set the Coke in front of me. "No, I don't remember you."

"Well, it was before I got struck. I looked different."

"No, I don't remember." She was starting away.

I stopped her. "What are you doing when you get off?"

"What do you want to know for?" Half turned, but stopped and waiting.

The blood rushed to my face. "I dunno, I thought maybe we could have a hamburger or something, you know, and talk. If you're not doing anything." It was hard getting it out.

"I don't know." She was thinking.

"What would it hurt?"

"I don't know." Her mouth changed into a crooked little smile. "What would anything hurt?"

"I could meet you somewhere."

"What kind of car you drive?"

"What kind of car?" I felt suddenly paralyzed. I couldn't think. "I don't have a car." It sounded so weak. I could feel myself shrinking.

"You don't have a car?" She couldn't believe it.

I shook my head.

"How do you expect to go on a date without a car?"

"I don't guess I do." I couldn't quite look at her.

"I don't guess you do either." She put her hands on her hips, a little angry. "How do you go anywhere?"

"Well, usually in a wagon."

"A wagon!" Her eyes really widened.

"But we lost our team." My words trailed off. I'd sounded like an imbecile.

She put my check down and walked away, shaking her head.

In another moment I slid off the stool and left as quietly as I could. I also left the check on the counter and purposely forgot to pay it.

Posters in the store windows advertised a May Day Festival coming soon, featuring a stock show, a carnival, a dance, a fair, and one other event that caught my eye. A mule-pulling contest. A small picture in the corner of the poster showed a wild team of white mules straining against a heavily loaded sled.

I imagined Judy and Mawd in that picture instead, but pulling that load easily. They'd pulled heavier timber in the hills. They were so well-matched and balanced it was almost uncanny and not like two separate animals. They pulled together so perfectly they were like a single engine with eight precision-tooled rods stabbing the ground. They'd reach with their necks, their bodies would slant forward, and when they were going good they were a wonderful sight. You could hold their reins lightly and direct them with the barest flick of the wrist. When you asked them to give all they had, they would.

Judy and Mawd could win that contest, and for a moment I envisioned the glory. We had made the final pull, and I was handed the prize, a golden trophy. The crowd was yelling and applauding and all eyes were on me. People were shaking my hand and patting me on the back. A beautiful girl was clinging to me and kissing my face. Then I was being interviewed on television. I said the other teams had been tough competition. I was modest. I wanted to give most of the credit to my team, to Judy and Mawd. I couldn't have done it without them.

But when I looked around, they were gone. The girl and the crowd vanished, and I was left standing alone.

I ate a meatloaf special at the City Cafe and went to the movie.

After that, I wandered the street, but purposefully. I pretended I was occupied with serious matters. I was only taking a break from important business and deep issues were on my mind. Anyone could see that. Some item in a store window would catch my eye and I would stop suddenly to see it better. To analyze it. It might be the missing piece to my project, the one thing I needed to complete my plans.

I asked a man on the street the time. He told me and I pretended to be late and hurried on. I had an appointment to close a big deal.

I went back to the cafe and paused as I entered to look around for the person who was supposed to be there waiting. I'd have to apologize for being late. But I didn't see him. I sat down and ordered coffee and kept my eye on the clock. When another person came in the door, I looked up expectantly and then acted disappointed. It wasn't my man. Finally I checked the time with the waitress, and when she said the clock was five minutes slow, that did it. I couldn't wait any longer. The guy who was supposed to meet me would just have to miss out.

I went to the back room of Dominoes.

Sailor was at a table in the far corner. It was fairly crowded, and when I approached, even when I got close, he didn't notice, so I stood and watched.

The game was draw poker and they were playing with money instead of chips. A hand had just been dealt and Sailor opened. Two men called and a third raised. Sailor—I knew he would—raised back. The two callers folded, but the first raiser said something under his breath and stayed.

The two of them then. Sailor drew one card, and the other man took two, saying he'd be honest.

Now they looked at each other. Sailor took a sip of whiskey from the glass at his elbow and grinned. It struck me how white his teeth showed. But his eyes were yellowish and red. The other man stared without expression and slipped his cards top to bottom, face down, in his hand.

Sailor had his cards cupped in one hand, sprung in

the top corner so he could see them without spreading them. He glanced at them and raised his eyebrows.

"I made it," he said, and bet.

The other man's expression didn't change. He started looking at his cards one tiny corner at a time, forcing each one to emerge only gradually, almost painfully, as if he were squeezing all the good he could out of them. It took him a long time to discover his hand, and then he looked at Sailor suspiciously, fondled his money, and again looked at his cards.

Finally he bet. And raised.

Sailor raised right back, saying, "I told you, I made it."

This time the man looked disgusted and angry. He brooded, tapped his cards and pulled at his ear. Then he said, "Okay, I call." He tossed out his money.

Sailor held his cards. "No raise?"

"C'mon, I called, whataya got?"

Sailor spread a bright diamond flush.

The man threw his cards down in a fit of temper and cursed. Three kings scattered. Then he reached his hand and stopped Sailor from raking in the pot. "Hey, wait a minute, let's see your openers."

Sailor showed them, a black jack he'd discarded and saved to the side, and the red jack in his hand. He had re-raised with that little pair and then split them to draw to a flush. Not a real good way to win at poker very often, but he had this time, and he had a big wad-ded pile of money in front of him from other winnings.

"You keep playing that way," the man said.

"I plan to." Sailor grinned and pulled in the pot.

As the cards were being dealt again, Sailor took another drink from his glass, a big swallow. He'd finish that glass pretty soon and get another, and as time passed, his eyes would gradually glaze over and his jaw would begin to sag. And then he'd start losing. That's the way it happened every time.

He noticed me. "What're you doing here?"

"Nothing."

"Then go someplace else."

"No place to go." I could see the cards in his hand, a bunch of little numbers in different colors. He discarded two and drew two more about the same.

"Go eat." He was betting.

"I already ate."

"Then go to the movie."

"I did."

Somebody raised and Sailor raised back. At the same time he said, "How 'bout a room, get one yet?"

"No."

He lost the hand and wasn't bothered. As the table was cleared, he tossed in another ante. "Okay, go get us a room at the Belvedere. Here." He fished a wrinkled twenty from the trashy pile in front of him and handed it to me.

I asked, "For the both of us?"

"Yeah." He was into his cards again.

"I oughta just pay for one, for myself."

"I'll be along. Pay for two."

"You coming?"

"When I finish here."

"I'll wait for you."

"No, you go on." He was betting.

"I won't bother anybody. I'll just sit and watch."

One of the other players noticed my face. "What happened to you?"

"I was struck by lightning." I pulled at my cap.

"Oh, yeah?" He wasn't impressed. "I had a cousin

2 9

once struck by lightning." He started talking to his cards. "Wasn't never quite the same after that, like it sorta shorted-out some of his wires. He'd see a woman on the street, he'd throw her down and pull off her shoes and start sucking on her toes. Had to watch him all the time."

Sailor was giving me the sign.

"Let me watch," I said. "What'll it hurt?"

"You're spoiling the rhythm."

"No, I'm not."

"Bud—" He gave me that look, and I knew he meant it.

At the door I looked back. Sailor was grinning at the other players in general, not quite seeing, and reaching for his drink. All that good money was heaped in front of him waiting to be lost. You could stick a match to it and watch it burn and it would be the same thing. Because, every time, Sailor lost. He'd do it on purpose—

The sudden thought startled me. *He'd do it on purpose.* So that was why it happened. The luck he had was him.

.   .   .

The Belvedere at one time had been a regular hotel, but now it was only a brick building with rooms on three floors. You registered at the waist-high counter across the first doorway in the hall.

"Ah, yes." The little man behind the counter looked up. "Back in town, are you? Bud, isn't it?" I was surprised he remembered my name. Sailor and I hadn't stayed at the Belvedere in months.

He stood up, and I became aware he was about my size, but he was thin and weak-looking. He had a flowering head of dark hair and thick horn-rimmed glasses. "How are you?" he said.

"Okay. Fine."

"It's good to see you again." He folded his hands on the counter between us, and they were little white delicate things sticking out of big French cuffs.

"Yeah, well, we just came in for the auction." I didn't want to be unfriendly, but I didn't like standing there either.

"Ah, the auction." He was pretending to be politely interested, but also out of politeness he was trying not to notice my face.

"Yeah, we lost our mules in the storm, and now we need to get a couple more."

"You lost your mules, oh, my."

"They ran off, you know, scared of the thunder and all."

"That's terrible."

"Yeah." His politeness was making me nervous. He was acting too nice. Then he smiled and that made it worse. His eyes were magnified behind his glasses and appeared weird when they shifted. They were round flat disks that floated.

"I guess I need a room." I laid the twenty on the counter.

He took the money, and then as if he shouldn't inquire, almost whispering, he said, "Just for yourself?"

I hesitated. But I knew Sailor wasn't coming. "Yeah, just for myself."

His expression was at once sad and sweet, enough to turn your stomach. "But Sailor's down the block," I said.

He straightened and changed his expression. "Yes, of course. Down the block." He counted out the ten dollars in change on the counter and picked a key from a side board. "I'm going to give you Number Four," he said, "right down the hall. You won't have to climb those old stairs."

"Okay." I didn't care. But when I reached for the key, he held onto it and I had to look at him.

His face was all screwed up, and he whispered, "You need a friend, don't you?"

How could he know? But it was so personal too. I just stood.

He released the key and smiled and patted my forearm. "My name's Lew. If you need anything, anything at all—I'm here."

I took the key and went to my room with my skin crawling. But I'm as big as he is, I thought, and I'm stronger. He's got little weak hands. If he tries anything, I'll kill him, I'll beat the shit out of him.

I lay down on the creaky bed and felt tired. It seemed I had been walking all day. But I needed to make some plans and definitely go somewhere and start a new life on my own. It was time. I needed to concentrate and figure out the steps, one, two, three. . . .

I woke. A soft knock at the door. "Bud?" Lew stuck his head in and saw me on the bed. "Oh, there you are. I forgot this." He came in with a towel. "You'll want to take a bath, I know."

I immediately sat up on the side of the bed.

He draped the towel on the chair and crossed to the window. "It's so stuffy in here, don't you think?" He raised the roller shade and the window halfway. "There, that's better."

He smiled. "How's the bed?"

"It's okay."

He felt of the mattress beside me, cautiously. "Oh, yes, nice and soft. You'll sleep like a log."

My stomach knotted. If he reached, I was ready. But that's all he did. He left quietly, closing the door behind him, and I listened to his footsteps going back down the hall, making tacky little sounds on the linoleum.

I took the towel and went to the bathroom down the hall the other way. I told myself I probably didn't have to worry.

But he did it again.

While I was in the tub, the door opened quietly. "Bud, are you there?" He didn't have to ask. He could see me sitting in plain sight. I almost jumped up, but I could see myself standing naked and exposed completely, so I held tight.

He eased into the room, holding out a bar of soap. "I didn't know if you had any soap."

"There's a bar right here."

"Oh, you don't want to use that old thing—here." He handed me a new bar and stood over me. His weird magnified eyes roved my body. Then he slowly leaned over and very carefully stuck his finger in the water near my leg. "Hot?"

"It's fine." I was braced, ready.

"You sure now?" He lingered.

"I told you, it's all right." The new soap in my hand was sweet smelling, but I was gripping it hard. I could slam it in his face and break his nose, knock his teeth out.

"Sometimes the hot water tank gets low and it takes a while to heat up." He pulled his hand away slowly and stood with a dripping finger and with his eyes still on me.

"The water's all right," I repeated.

"I just wanted to check and make sure."

I waited. The air was heavy.

"I'm sorry you lost your mules," he said.

"Yeah, me too."

It seemed it was all he could do to pull himself away and leave. He forced a smile and looked hurt.

At the door he stopped and gave a little wave with his hand bending at the wrist. "Have a nice bath," he said, and again I heard his steps going away, sticking to the linoleum.

A swoosh of air came out of me. I didn't realize I had been holding my breath, and I finished washing as fast as I could. But not with the new soap he'd brought. It was too scented and slick. I used the old bar I'd had to begin with.

Then, washed and clean, I put on my old clothes and combed my hair. And that was it. That's all I could help. My face in the mirror was a bald mask. I couldn't tell it was me, only that it was my eyes looking through cut-out holes. My only hope was to pretend I was in some sort of disguise.

Going out, I bent over to sneak past Lew's counter.

.   .   .

It was night and the town was quiet. Only a few cars idly roamed the main street. The pool hall was nearly empty, and the nearest service station looked vacant.

I went into a phone booth and made up a number and dialed. A phone was such an opposite thing than what it appeared. It really allowed you to see more than hear, but you could hide with it and not be seen yourself.

The phone rang and someone answered, "Hello." A soft voice, a woman's.

I didn't say anything.

"Hello?"

"Yuh." I made the sound short and deep in my throat.

"Bill? Is that you, Bill?"

"Yuh." The same sound again.

"You sound funny. What's the matter?" I could see her lying in bed in a blue satin nightgown, one knee up, her long hair on her pillow.

I made another sound, not exactly a word.

"Where are you? I've been waiting."

I tried not to breathe. Her lips were full and moist near my ear. Her eyes were soft and filled with longing.

"Bill?"

"Yuh."

"What's the matter? Can't you talk?"

"Uh-hmm." She was sitting up now, concerned, her white shoulders bare in the lamplight. Her arms cradled her beautiful breasts.

Her voice dropped. "Is *she* listening?"

I made another sound.

"She is." Now she whispered, "You can't get away? You can't come?"

I didn't answer.

"No?" A sad plaintive word, and I could imagine her face, her feelings. She drew a tiny breath. "I want you, honey, I miss you."

Bill was a bastard.

"I'm going to lock the door," she said. "You know I'm afraid at night if I don't, if you're not coming."

I saw her later asleep in the dark. She had locked the door, and someone was rattling it, trying to get in.

It was Bill, but she didn't know that, and she was scared.

"Don't," I said.

"What?"

"Don't lock your door. You don't have to be afraid. Bill's coming." I hung up.

Now, I didn't know it, and wouldn't for a long time, but what was about to happen was already in place. All the pieces were there and waiting, and I can name them now. Our axes. Our mules. The woods. The river rats. The town and Lew. The whores and gambling. Sailor with his violent and misfit nature. Me with my yearnings and imagination—and one other person.

I look back on it now, and it seems both inevitable and a fluke. That one other person was the spark that lit the fuse. But it started as a coincidence. For no particular reason I happened to be in a random spot at a certain time. And that was pure accident. I could have been in that spot at a different time, a minute earlier or later even, and nothing would have happened.

But the fact is, I was there, the other ingredients had piled up, she came along, and the rest followed.

It was after the blind phone call. Again I had nothing to do and I decided to walk to the roller rink at the edge of town. The rink was a tent affair with rolled-up sides and rough flooring, and when I got there skaters were going round and round and I stood at the rail and watched.

It occurs to me now, once you've seen skating for an instant, you've seen it forever, and yet you can watch it endlessly. Maybe it's the continuous circling, the going around and always ending up back where you started, and that's something close to the cycles in life and seasons. I don't know, but you can think of it as a sport too and make a show of it and pretend what you're doing in your own circling is different and better than anyone else's.

For a time, in my mind, I was in the rink spinning and doing tricks with my feet. Everybody was watching and especially one girl. She was smiling at me each time I passed, and after a time, after a swerving turn as smooth as glass, I glided by and swept her away.

She was wearing white skate boots and a short skirt and I had my arm around her waist. She was light as a feather. I lifted her above my head and spun around and brought her body sliding down against mine. I dipped her back until her hair skimmed the floor. It was like a dream and we never seemed to breathe and we skated perfectly together. The music changed to a waltz and we danced slowly and gracefully round and round. We were in love.

I left the rink and started walking along the highway back to town. It was late and there was no moon, so it was dark too, but I made out a car ahead of me poking along, its motor idling. This was the random spot and moment, the coincidence. The car's taillights showed it was green, and I could see the driver was leaning across the seat and talking out the window on the passenger's side. A girl was walking along the shoulder of the highway and that's why the car was slowed down to keep pace. The guy was trying to get the girl to stop, but she wasn't listening. He was trying to pick her up or she'd gotten out and wouldn't ride with him anymore. She was walking hard. He finally pulled up a little ahead of her and opened the door, but she marched right by. With the door open, the interior light showed him dressed in a soldier's uniform.

He caught up with her again in the car, and this time she picked up a rock and threw it at his windshield. It hit the rounded corner and glanced off. I didn't hear a shatter. But that's all it took. The soldier immediately gunned the motor, spun his wheels, and roared off. The girl was picking up another rock but she was left in a swirl at the roadside.

My heart jumped. I knew who it was and I ran toward her, yelling, "Hey!"

2

Hominy turned. "Who's that?"

"It's me, Bud, remember?" I trotted up to her.

"Leave me alone." She whirled to walk away and slipped in the gravel. I reached to help her and she pushed me off. "I said leave me alone!"

"I was just trying to catch you."

"I can catch myself."

"Okay, I'm sorry."

"You creep!"

"I said I was sorry."

"What're you doing here anyway?"

"Nothing. I was watching—"

"Then go away." She started on, walking hard, her face thrust forward into the night.

I followed. The direction she was taking, back to town, was my direction too. But she could hear my steps behind her, and after a short distance, she halted and turned with her hands on her hips. "Okay, what-aya want?"

"Nothing." I had stopped too, and we were about ten steps apart. "I'm going this way too."

"What're you doing back there?"

"Nothing."

A pause. I could feel her glaring at me through the dark. Then she resigned herself. "All right," she sighed. "Come on."

I hurried to her and we started walking side by side. It was almost as if we were together and I felt light on my feet, even lighter in my head. I'd never walked with a girl before, not in real life.

"I'm mad," she said.

"What happened?"

"None of your business."

"That guy in the car—"

"The bastard."

"What'd he do?"

"I told you, none of your business."

She was walking angrily and breathing hard. I peeked sideways to see if her clothes were torn, to see if she'd had to fight, but I couldn't see anything wrong. She was wearing tight jeans and a red shirt that was unbuttoned at the neck just far enough to show the start of her breasts.

A car approached and we moved off the shoulder.

It passed with a roar and swoosh of air, and I thought it might have been a green car and the soldier again.

"Your boyfriend—" I started to say.

But she cut me off. "I don't have a boyfriend."

That surprised me. "You don't?"

"I have a date with some asshole, that don't make 'em a boyfriend."

"No, I guess not."

"I don't want to talk to you no more either."

We tramped on in silence except for the sound of our shoes in the gravel.

Then the drive-in was before us, its neon light blinking. "Hey," I said, "How 'bout a hamburger?"

"And sneak out without paying?"

"Whataya mean?"

"You sneaked out on your Cokes, didn't you?"

"When?" I couldn't admit it.

"Don't gimme that bull." She turned on me. "You don't even have a car!"

That nailed me.

"Look at us," she said, "out here nowhere having to walk!"

"I don't mind walking, though."

"It's humiliating!" She turned her back and repeated it. "Humiliating." Then she was holding herself, and her shoulders were shaking. I thought she was crying and I felt helpless. With her back to me she appeared such a sad and lonely thing. I wanted to enfold her somehow and absorb her body into mine.

I stepped close and touched her arm. She was making little sounds that wanted to cry but she was holding back. Or maybe she couldn't cry. She clutched at my arm to steady herself, released and clutched again, and I felt strong. No one had ever held on to me, and it was a curious thing. It was a strange and warm sensation.

She smelled clean and fresh.

"I don't think you broke his windshield," I said. "I think the rock just glanced off."

She shook her head and gained control. "At least he had a car."

"Well, anyway," I said, "are you all right?"

She bared her teeth. "I'm always all right."

"Let's get a hamburger."

"I don't want one."

"I'm hungry."

"I'm not." But she came with me anyway.

Then the lighted drive-in area revealed us and we both became stiff and walked more rigidly, hardly moving our arms. Hominy held her chin higher and combed at her hair with her fingers. I pulled at my cap and became consicous of my face. Instead of driving up naturally in a car, private and half hidden, the way you're supposed to, we were walking in from out of nowhere for all the world to see, and we were exposed.

By myself, I wouldn't have cared. That's what I did alone and I could pretend to be on the prowl, but with a girl, with Hominy, it definitely made us objects to be stared at and I could tell she felt that.

We got through the cars hung with trays, to the door to go inside, and Hominy stopped. "You go on in," she said. "I gotta go to the rest room a minute."

Idiotically, I must have tried to follow.

She pushed me back. "What're you doing? I gotta comb my hair. Now go on."

I went on inside then and picked a table near the window. I wanted to be able to see her come out, but the rest rooms were around the corner and out of sight. Which meant she could slip away without me seeing and I had a funny feeling she wanted to do just that.

Still, I ordered two hamburgers and Cokes and waited. There were eight other tables in the place, a jukebox, and two pinball machines, but no other customers. I passed the time trying to stack the salt and pepper shakers on top of the catsup bottle.

After about ten minutes, when the hamburgers came but Hominy didn't, I went outside to check. The ladies' room door, naturally, was closed, but I walked by and tried to listen. I heard a sound. Someone was in there, and as I passed, a girl came out, but it wasn't Hominy, and I walked by again. This time there was no sound behind the door except the final squeezing-off of the water in the commode.

The area behind the drive-in was dark. There was a flat stretch of vacancy before the town began and in that space nothing moved. I looked for some form or shadow hurrying away, but she had disappeared completely.

What did you expect, I told myself, she wasn't even friendly.

But she had almost cried and held on to me for support, and it had been a good feeling. I spent a long moment staring off into the night.

Then I went back inside and sat down with the two hamburgers. They were getting cold, and I didn't want them, but I picked one up and crammed my mouth with it and chewed. And this was me, a mouth with no face chewing. Two eyes looking through cut-out holes in a blank mask.

In my mind the green car had picked her up again.

It had come along and stopped in the vacancy back there, and this time, when he opened the door for her, she'd gotten in. The soldier'd smirked at her. "I knew you'd come around." And she'd replied, "You win, I'm yours now, you can do what you want." They were going to some spot to park and he was going to rip her red shirt open and she'd have to take it. Then he was going to be all over her like a dog.

That's what I was thinking, imagining, when I felt someone standing to my side and a little back. My mouth was full of hamburger, and I stopped chewing when I looked.

"I decided to come back," she said.

"Yeah?" I managed to swallow. "What for?"

She shrugged.

·   ·   ·

She told me she had quit school at the beginning of the eighth grade the year before and left home. She was fifteen. "But I tell people I'm sixteen to stay outta trouble. You know, fifteen, they still mess with you about school."

After the hamburgers we'd walked to the house where she rented a room. "Seventeen dollars a week, but it's a big room and it's all mine." We didn't go in, but sat on the back steps facing the alley. A big screened porch was behind us.

She was talking, "—nine of us living in two rooms, crap all over the place. Yelling and screaming all the time. I used to go off and hide just to get away from it, just for a little privacy."

She was sitting with her knees up and her arms resting across them and there was no doubt in my mind, at that moment, she was the most beautiful girl I'd ever seen. There was still no moon and the back of the house was darkened but I could see her profile in shadow and starlight. Her nose was straight, her chin was small and rounded, and her mouth was perfect. Her pretty teeth flashed in the night and I couldn't stop looking at her. There was also a glint in her eyes like the pip of a tiny searchlight and her eyes were such moving things. They were so restless and seeking, it seemed. Only I wished her hair was longer. It was short like a boy's.

"People ask me where I got my ideas," she said, "but I was always comparing and I always wanted things better. Living out in the country, growing up that way, I hated it. We never had nothing."

"Never had anything," I corrected her without thinking.

"That's what I said."

"No, you said never had nothing, and that's wrong. That's a double negative."

She looked at me. "What's a double negative?"

"Nothing. It doesn't matter." I didn't want her to think I was criticizing.

"I want to know."

"No, really, it doesn't matter."

"You think you talk better'n me?"

"I didn't mean it. I'm sorry I said anything."

"But you did. And now I want to know. What's a damn double negelly or whatever?" She wasn't going to let it go.

I took a deep breath, "Okay, a double negative. That's when you put two no words together, like not never."

"I didn't say not never."

"You said never nothing, same thing."

"I said never *had* nothing."

"But you still said never and nothing in the same sentence and you can't do that."

She eyed me. "Where'd you learn that?"

"Out of books."

She looked away, and I was glad to let it rest.

I had been in school here and there, but we were always moving and I didn't like school. As soon as I made a friend, we'd move and I'd have to leave the friend behind and that was the thing that got to me pretty quick. School very shortly became a place where you found someone you knew you'd also have to forget. So I finally quit going to school entirely. But Sailor saw to it that I studied. He'd get the books I was supposed to have for the year and I'd do my lessons at night. And, truthfully, I didn't mind. My lessons were easy. I'd go through some books, Sailor would find me more, and by the time I was thirteen and supposedly in the seventh grade, I was really in high school. I liked reading. And the meaning of words. Sailor understood. "But just remember," he'd say, "the meaning of words can only take you so far. You gotta have some understanding on your own apart from words."

Hominy finally spoke, softly. "You know, you're funny."

"Yeh, I guess I am." An oddball, a quirk.

"I mean, you seem older'n just thirteen."

"I wish I were."

"No, it's okay." Quiet, reassuring words. The arguing over. I felt something rising between us, feelings of warmth spiraling up.

"I need to learn to talk right. I want you to teach me." She faced me, her face tight. "Will you?"

"Sure, if I can." I felt embarrassed. "I mean, I don't talk right a lot myself."

"But you know how. And I need to learn."

"I just know what I read."

"That's more'n me." Now she pulled back a little and squared herself at me. "But you'd teach me just as a friend, that's all."

"Well, sure, whatever." I knew what she meant, and she didn't have to insist. A friend was enough.

"I gotta do better. I've never been nothing," she said.

"I know what you mean."

"My family was nothing but trash."

"Not trash," I said.

"Yeh, we were. My pa never worked at nothing. My brothers neither. They ran a still, and when we had money that's where it come from, bootlegging. But they never give me none. My momma coughed herself to death when I was ten, and that's how I got my first pair of shoes. They took 'em off her when they buried her and give 'em to me."

She was wearing sandals and they were small and neat. Her toenails were nicely polished. But I saw her feet also in some old woman's shoes too big for her and run down at the heels.

"I had one ol' raggedy dress for school."

I could see her in that too.

"I had to keep letting the hem out." Now she waved her hand away and abruptly changed her tone. "I'm not trying to feel sorry for myself. That's just the way it was. But that's all behind me now, and I ain't never gonna live that way again. Never." Her jaw was set.

I didn't know how she could sound so tough and look so pretty.

I said, "So you don't see your folks anymore?"

"No." She turned her face away. Then she admitted, "Just one of my brothers. He keeps coming around."

"And you don't want him to?"

"I can't keep him off." Bitterly.

I didn't know what to say. If she wanted me to, I'd keep him away. I'd stand up to him. But I didn't know how to say that and make it sound right.

"I gotta get away from here too." She dropped her hands between her thighs. "If I had the money, I'd pack my clothes and leave this minute." She looked at the sky. "I'd go to Dallas. Maybe stop off in Little Rock. But Dallas is where all the money is, all the oil and stuff."

"That's pretty far, though." I couldn't imagine it.

"You don't think I can get there?" She cut her eyes at me.

"No, I believe you can."

"When I save the money, I'm going to do it."

And me too, I thought. I didn't want to be left behind.

She went on, "I've got it figured. I got away to here, and I'm working and I'm making it here, but this is nothing. This is just the first step. The next step is Dallas. And then I keep going till I make it all the way."

All the way. It sounded good. But all the way where? "Till you live like you want to," I said.

"You go one step at a time. If it takes awhile, that's okay. You keep the end in sight and keep going, one step at a time."

"And you make plans." I was with her.

"You don't let yourself get sidetracked."

"I'm taking steps myself. I'm going to clear outta here too."

"Oh, yeh?" She confronted me. "When're you going?"

I was suddenly stopped. Someone was taking me at my word matter-of-factly and waiting for an answer.

I cleared my throat. "Well, I don't know. I gotta close a deal first." I didn't know why I had to say that. I shouldn't have.

"What kinda deal?"

"Well, it's kinda secret. I'm not supposed to talk about it." I knew I sounded stupid. I was going to ruin myself with her.

A corner of her mouth went up, and that provoked me.

"You don't have to believe me."

"Don't worry, I don't."

"Then you just wait. This deal's going to be worth a lot of money. I've been working on it for about a year now." She was already looking bored, but I kept on. "It's the kind of deal I've been waiting for, a real money deal, and I've got to handle it just right." I clamped my mouth.

She waited.

"And you're right," I said. "I don't have a deal."

"I know you don't."

"I don't know why I said it." I felt defeated.

"You wanted to sound like a big shot."

"I guess." I couldn't quite look at her. I had embarrassed myself.

"Hey"—she touched my knee—"it's okay."

That made me feel better. I wanted to touch her back. But she was suddenly tense and listening for something in the dark. She grabbed my arm.

"What is it?"

"Be quiet," she whispered, and cocked her ear for some sound in the bushes along the driveway, but as far as the alley nothing moved. The only sound was a cricket and the faint purr of a faraway car.

"Come in with me." She kept her voice low and pulled at my arm. "I want you to stay with me, just for a little while." Her grasp tightened, an urgency. "Okay?"

"You want me to?" She'd made me sound needed.

"We gotta be quiet, though. My landlady sleeps in the front."

She opened the squeaky screen door cautiously and led me tiptoeing across the porch, down the hall a few steps and into her room, all in the dark.

She left the light off in her room and pulled me down quietly to sit beside her on the edge of the bed. For some time we were silent and still, side by side. As my eyes adjusted, I made out a dresser against the wall, a table and chair and a nightstand. And empty space. There was a rug on the floor, and I had an impression of neatness and order, a tidy sort of simplicity. There was also a fresh smell in the air, the scent of flowers somewhere. It was a room that was cared for and the bed was deep and soft.

I whispered, "What did you hear, that soldier?"

"No, not him."

"You were scared of something."

"You don't have to know." She moved up on the bed and sat against the headboard. I could see her as a form but not distinctly. "Just stay a little while longer and then you can go."

I tried to rest with my elbows on my knees. I was alone with a girl in her room. We were in the dark and on her bed. It was almost another world.

I whispered, "If you want me to, I can go out there and look around, make sure."

"No, I don't want you to do that."

"It'll be okay." I started to get to my feet.

"No!" She grabbed my sleeve. "Don't, please." It was a plea. "Come here." She pulled at me, and I scooted up beside her. "Now"—she patted my knee— "you just stay right here."

We sat together against the headboard, our shoulders and hips touching delicately.

"You know what you heard," I said. "Not the soldier, but somebody else?"

"It doesn't matter. Be quiet."

"An old boyfriend?"

"No."

"Who then?"

"It's none of your business."

"But if he scares you—"

"Stop it—he don't scare me. I just don't like him bothering me—screwing me up." Her teeth clenched. "I'm through with all that now."

She had tightened. Then I felt her give up and sag. Her hands were lying palms up in her lap in a helpless fashion and she was looking down at them, her eyes fixed. She might have been a puppet or doll that had been laid aside without regard. She could have been something thrown away and forgotten.

I wanted to put my arm around her and hold her hand, but I was afraid she would pull away entirely and leave me with nothing. We were touching still at the shoulders.

Then I decided she was okay. We all had our own feelings, and I was content just being with her, and I wanted it to be forever nice and quiet, the two of us. We could make it together. With our eyes closed . . .

Hominy was nudging me, "Okay, you can go now."

I didn't want to move.

"C'mon." She patted my knee.

I scooted down from the headboard until I was stretched out on my back.

"Hey, c'mon." She still spoke quietly.

"Do I have to?"

"You can't stay here all night."

"I was feeling peaceful."

"I gotta be careful of my landlady. C'mon."

"Okay." But I didn't raise. I crossed my arms across my chest.

Hominy was sitting on the edge of the bed. "You're going to get me in trouble, you know that?"

"You asked me to come in."

"But just for a while."

"What if somebody's still out there?"

"They're not."

"How do you know?"

"'Cause by now he thinks you're staying, and it wouldn't do him any good."

"Didn't do me any good either."

I think her lip curled. Her eyes sparked.

"I just like being with you," I said. "I hate to leave."

"You're gonna start a fight and wake my landlady."

"No, I won't."

A moment passed. Then she cocked her head. "You a cherry?"

I couldn't answer.

"You are, ain'tcha?"

I still couldn't answer.

She eyed me and shook her head slowly. "What'm I gonna do with you?" Or us, I thought.

Then she reached for me. "Okay, you just lay there."

Her hand touched my leg. "You don't have to do nothing," she said. Her hand moved along my thigh and found my crotch. She squeezed and I sat up, bolt upright, but she pushed me back. "No, be still," she said.

Her hand glided on my fly and I closed my eyes. She was massaging gently and I felt myself growing. Little spots were racing in my mind. Her palm was flat against me and moving up and down and soon it was too much. I raised again and tried to put my arms around her but she held me off again. "Don't, now, just lay there."

"I want to kiss you."

"I don't want you to."

I fell back with my arms across my face and she continued. I felt my body rising and my legs straightened. I think I was trembling. Her hand closed around me through my pants and stroked faster. I could hear myself breathing and she was leaning against me, breathing with me. There was a tingling in my thighs. A hot flash started in my hips and began to spread. She was asking, "You never had this done before?" and I was shaking my head, and then it was there.

"Now you gotta go." She got up.

I was lying in a dream.

"It's late, c'mon." She was at the door waiting.

I sat up. The room was chilly now and there was a stickiness in my pants.

"C'mon." She was impatient.

"Okay, okay." I stood up, but I still didn't want to leave. It had happened too quick and my feelings were left hanging. There needed to be something more, something said. I didn't know what. We'd never kissed. We'd never held hands.

She pulled me by the sleeve through the door and across the porch.

"You don't have to drag me," I said.

"You stayed long enough." She pushed me at the steps.

This time I didn't like being pushed and I threw her arm away. "Just a minute!"

But she pushed again. "Go."

I stopped two steps down and turned. "I don't get it."

She was above me, pulling the screen door closed, but I blocked it. "What did I do?"

She let go of the door. "You gonna make me mad."

"I'm going to leave, but I don't get it."

She made a gesture of exasperation. "Look, I figured you were trying to act nice, walking me home, so I paid you back, okay?"

"You didn't have to do that. I didn't ask you to."

"You wanted to get your rocks off, you did."

"I wanted to kiss you."

"Kiss me!"

"You wouldn't let me."

"Why would I? I don't even know you."

"Hominy—I love you." I didn't know I was going to say that. She was so beautiful above me on the gloomy porch, her eyes glinting, her teeth flashing.

She was also suddenly frozen as if I'd slapped her. Her mouth opened and closed.

"I do," I said.

"No." She managed to speak.

"Ever since I first saw you."

Now she gathered herself. "I don't want to hear that crap."

"I mean it."

"I don't go for that."

"Just the same—"

"Just get outta here, will ya? I don't want you around." She was pushing me again and trying to close the screen door between us.

I moved. "You don't have to like me back—"

"That's for damn sure, I don't." She pulled the door tight and latched it in my face. I could barely see her behind the screen. "Besides," she said, "you're too young for me."

"You said I could teach you, though. You still want me to, I could."

She didn't answer.

"You know, double negatives."

"You oughta do something about your face."

"I'm hoping it'll grow back."

"It needs something." She had moved back from the door and I couldn't see her at all now.

I put my face to the screen and peered in, but I still couldn't see her. "Hominy—?"

No answer.

Then from the dark, a small voice: "Didja mean it?"

"What?"

The door to the house closed quickly.

I called after her, "Wait, I did, I meant it—Hominy?" But she was gone. There was total silence, and I was left with my nose against the screen.

You don't have to like me back, I thought. I don't care—

Moments later I was hit in the head with a rock. I was walking in the drive to the street and the night was carrying me. We'd been alone together and I knew exactly what her bed felt like, deep and soft and springy, and the spread had been smooth and tight. There had been the scent of flowers and the room was a privacy. A different world—

Then I was hit in the back of the head and I saw the rock bouncing in the drive. It had been thrown hard and ricocheted from my shoulder, fist size.

I whirled and caught a glimpse of something darting in the bushes, in the alley, a shadow, but it was out of sight before I could see.

I picked up a stick and started backing to the street. They were still there. I felt that. They were hiding and watching. Any second they'd lunge at me. Some warped thing would drop from the trees. The drive was too narrow and the stick was no good, too light and brittle.

I felt the back of my head and my fingers came away wet. Blood was trickling down my neck.

When I got to the street, I kept backing and I didn't stop. I threw the stick and ran.

.   .   .

Lew was swabbing my head. He'd seen the blood when I came in and pulled me into his office, and I was sitting in his chair.

"It must hurt." He was behind me with the pan of water and a washcloth. My hair was clotted where he dabbed.

"It's just sorta throbbing now."

"It looks bad. But the bleeding's stopped."

His fingers were so dainty back there, and I couldn't see him, but I could smell him, like he was powdered with some kind of heavy talcum, and his breath was funny, as if he'd gargled with stale cologne. There was no ordinary or natural scent about him.

"You should see a doctor."

"I'll be okay." But I jerked my head. He'd touched a spot that hurt.

"Sorry." His fingers became even daintier. "You should go to the hospital and get this dressed properly. Let them look at it."

"Just hurry, okay? I'm getting tired of sitting." I didn't like the way he was mincing with the cloth and I wasn't used to someone fussing over me.

"Your scalp is split. It may need stitches."

"I don't want stitches."

"And you don't know who did it?" He kept dabbing.

"I turned around, I thought I saw something, but it was dark and I couldn't see. They must've just thrown the rock and run."

"And you don't know why? No reason?"

"I wasn't doing anything."

"There." He finished with the cloth. "I'll put something on it."

"That's all right." I wanted to leave.

"No, sit, sit." He pressed my shoulders back down and went into the next room.

I felt of my head. My hair was damp but the dried blood was gone. What was left was an open gash across a big lump and it was tender to the touch, a little aching all over. It had been a good rock.

Lew returned with a disinfectant and a box of bandages. I didn't want a bandage. That would only make me more noticeable and call attention to my face.

"But it'll keep the dirt out," he said.

"I don't care."

He sprayed the disinfectant. "You really ought to see a doctor."

"I don't like doctors."

"This happened over a girl, didn't it?"

"Whataya mean?" I straightened. He was still behind me.

"I bet it did."

"I told you, I was just walking along, not doing anything."

"But you like girls, don't you?" He was still spraying.

"That ought to be enough."

"Almost." He sprayed—*psst, psst*—one hand on my shoulder, moving.

I stood up. "That's enough."

His eyes were not in his head. They were magnified disks inside his glasses. "Don't get mad." His cologne breath was in the air.

I stepped back, and he stepped sideways, and the space between us remained the same, about an arm's length. His eyes were floating. "What's wrong?"

"I'm going."

"I think you misunderstood me."

"I know you." I was ready.

"Bud, listen, I like you. I want to be a friend, that's all."

"You're a queer."

"I knew you'd think that." He wasn't fazed.

"You better get outta my way." I knew I could take

him. He was so frail-looking. And I wanted to hit him. I think I had my fist ready.

But he only shrugged and moved back like a little bird with folded wings. His thin fingers sticking out of his big French cuffs were his wing feathers.

I walked past him and went to my room, left my clothes where they fell, and crawled into bed.

As soon as I lay down, I started breathing as if I'd run all day. I was dead tired. But I couldn't sleep on my back, on my lump. I had to turn onto my side.

Sometime in the night Sailor was looking down at me, feeling of my head. Lew was standing in the doorway, but I wasn't awake. The way Sailor roughed over my head hurt.

"He's all right." Sailor's voice. Slurry. Drunk.

Then his voice was leaving, talking to Lew. "Hell, you made it sound like he was dying."

"It looked bad." Lew's voice. Small. Worried.

"Nah, just a bump."

Lights out.

.   .   .

The next morning when I pressed my lump, it hurt, but it wasn't bad to touch. I sat up and felt dizzy, then the dizziness passed and I was all right. Except I couldn't find my clothes.

I remembered dropping them on the floor but they weren't there. What if the rock had ruined the memory spot in my brain? What if it had smashed the key cell that held my mind together and left me stupid? They had operations that zapped a tiny dot in the brain and turned people into zombies, and that's what the rock could have done to me—turned me into an idiot that was always losing his clothes, that was always running around naked.

But that's not what happened.

I found my clothes hanging in the closet, and the first sight of them seemingly suspended in air gave me a peculiar feeling. The quiet space around me had been secretly penetrated in the night. The clothes had been very neatly hung and separated, and a quality of deftness still prevailed. A kind of deception was hanging there too.

I brought my shirt and pants out one at a time and held them to the light. For a second I didn't think they were mine. They'd been washed and ironed, perfectly clean.

I stopped at Lew's counter on my way out.

He was reading a paper and looked up. "Ah, there you are. How's your head?"

"It's okay."

"Oh, good, I'm glad." His face lit up.

And I let go. "Look, these are my clothes, understand? My own personal clothes that I wear. When they need washing, I'll do it myself. I don't want your fruity hands touching them, understand?"

His face fell, his enlarged eyes blinked, and his mouth twitched. "I was only trying—"

"I don't care what you were trying. I don't like you sneaking in on me everywhere. Now, I mean it."

I thought he was going to cry, and I wasn't about to watch that, so I left.

The next thing I knew, I saw the future. Or, at least, some part of it.

I was heading for the drugstore, walking along and not thinking. The morning was clear and sunny, an ordinary day. Lew was behind me and forgotten. There was the normal small-town laziness in the streets and the usual traffic. I was probably feeling of my eyebrows to see if they were growing again. I was trying to imagine a spriggle of new hairs.

All at once I saw my life was about to become complicated and changed. Things were going to happen. In a flash I saw whole images and it was more than a premonition. It was a picture, a wide view, and it gave me a certain knowledge, not in details and specifics, but overall. I saw. Judy and Mawd were waiting. An ax was raised. Hominy was damaged. Sailor was dying. I had a new face.

Then it was gone. The picture vanished.

I might have stopped. I think I was supposed to. And someone else might have altered his course right then, but that wasn't me. I was bound in my direction.

I went on and crossed the street.

There's no such thing as nearly. It either happens or it doesn't, and you forget it. That's what Sailor said. You can't go back. Still, there's that old longing deep down for what might have been, for what should have been, and it's with me always.

The green car stopped in front of the drugstore in the middle of the block and Hominy got out. I was on the corner. She was wearing her uniform and carrying her apron and it seemed she was still closing the door when the car drove away. The soldier behind the wheel hadn't given her a second glance, as if he'd used her, was through with her now, and he couldn't get rid of her fast enough. I couldn't see the expression on her face. She walked into the drugstore with a toss of her head.

That guy had tried something the night before, and she had gotten out and walked instead, but now he was back, in broad daylight and out in the open. I think the blood drained to my feet.

I sat on the end stool and she waited on me. The regular customers had their places down the counter.

"I thought you didn't like him," I said.

"Who?" Her eyes were smudged and a little red, but she was still pretty.

"That guy, that soldier."

"What about him?" She took a casual stance.

"I saw you get out of his car."

"He gave me a ride to work—so?"

"So I guess you like him."

"What's it to you?"

"I was just asking."

"Suppose it's none of your business?"

"You said you didn't have a boyfriend." I had no rights, but I'd had hopes, that was the thing.

Her expression was caught between feelings. We knew each other and didn't. She could get mad or ignore me. What was it worth? And this wasn't the place for anything. "Look, I'm not going to just stand here. You want something, or what?"

"Some coffee."

She moved away, gliding, perfectly balanced, and that left me unsettled. I had an odd feeling I was in the middle of a story. I had skipped the beginning, and I didn't know who the characters were, but I was supposed to.

She spilled the coffee in my saucer, setting it down. "Oh, sorry."

"Hominy." I caught her eye. "Last night—"

"Forget last night." She moved away again.

And forget the soldier too, I thought.

I poured the coffee in the saucer back in my cup. The soldier didn't matter. He'd given her a ride, trying to make up, but she wouldn't give him another date and that's why he drove away mad. I could let it go.

I gave myself some business with the cream and sugar, the stirring and sipping—I pretended I was thinking.

Between customers and refills, we talked.

I asked, "Still plan on going to Dallas?"

"I told you I was, didn't I?"

"When do you think you'll go?"

"Soon's I save enough money."

"How much do you think you'll need?"

"I figure five hundred."

"Dollars?"

"I'm going to get me an apartment, though, not just another room. And I'm going to get me some nice clothes. I told you, Dallas is the next step, and I'm stepping up."

I saw her leaving with a suitcase, getting on a bus.

"What are you going to do when you get there?" I asked.

"I'm going to be a hostess. Maybe not right off. But I'm not going to wait tables all my life. I want to get me a job as a hostess in a nice place where I greet people when they come in and take 'em to their tables, and everybody has to dress up to get in. Then after that I'm going to have a nice house and travel around the world."

"You could marry somebody rich and it'd be easy."

"I'm going to do it myself."

"It sounds like a lot."

"You gotta think big." The corner of her mouth up.

She asked me, "You got any plans?"

"Well, I guess I just want to live in town somewhere, like other people."

"Is that all?"

"I guess I'm a couple steps behind you."

"I coulda told you that." Almost laughing, but prettily.

"Ya know something?" She was thoughtful now, lingering. "I talk to you, don't I? I just asked myself, why am I talking to you?" Shaking her head. "I don't tell nobody nothing, you know what I mean? I don't want to. But I've been telling you. I've already told you more about me than I ever told anybody—why do you reckon I do?"

"Maybe you just want to."

"Maybe I kinda like you." Gauging me.

"Well, I like you." A little embarrassed, but not bad.

"But I keep thinking, you know, you're younger'n me."

"Next month I'll be a year older."

"And you don't know nothing about girls."

"I could learn, though."

"You don't even have a face."

"I will, though. I can feel it underneath right now, trying to grow back."

She brought my check. "And you better pay this one," she said. Then she added, "I get off at five. You want to, I'll meet you by the river."

That was a moment. She told me where.

The woman behind the cash register smiled. "I think this one's yours too." The check for the Cokes the day before. "I'm sure you just forgot."

"Well, not exactly." I gave her the money.

"Oh, I know, sometimes a person's not thinking, and they walk out, but they don't mean it." Still smiling.

"No, I did it on purpose."

Her smile faded, and I walked out happy.

I'd forgotten to tell Hominy about the rock and show her my lump, but I could do that down by the river.

·　　　·　　　·

I was going to tell Sailor too, I'd made up my mind. I was going to stay in town and find a job and save some money and go to Dallas with Hominy.

I wouldn't tell him about Hominy, of course, but I was going to have my own life now and go my separate way. He could do without me and I could do without him, and it was about time. He didn't care anyway. He could stay in the trees and live alone and be a stranger to every living soul forever, that's all he wanted. But I was going to be with people and live normal because that's what I wanted. I'd get me a job with some company and work my way up. I'd work overtime and when it was Christmas I wouldn't let it pass. I'd get a car.

I'd made up my mind.

But it was still morning and Sailor would still be at Pauline's. I didn't have to think twice about that. He would have gone there drunk in the night and stayed. I know now it couldn't have been much. About the most he did, probably, was give them his money and pass out, and they'd let him lie there somewhere and sleep it off.

But that's where he'd be. Then maybe he'd make it to the auction and I could see him there.

Since the auction wouldn't start until noon, I went by the hardware store to look around and that was always an interesting place to me. They had so many little things that fitted into bigger things, you could imagine the really intricate way the world worked. All the parts were there that made up civilization, that you needed to keep civilization running and repaired. You could start with a screw, add a washer, a piece of metal, a nut and bolt, and keep on until you'd built some machine or battleship. You could start with a wheel and end up with a car. A rifle is probably what happened to the spear. You could take something plain and simple and add to it, and pretty soon you'd have yourself a whole new world, or even an invention. All you needed was the right kind of brains.

That's why I liked hardware stores. But this time, after wandering around, I went to the garden department and swiped a package of seeds from the rack. Kentucky Wonder green beans, the kind you don't have to string. And I don't know why I did that, but that's the way you start a garden and make things grow, and a garden is full of dreams.

I still had time and I was looking again at the poster in the window, the one about the May Day Festival with the picture of the white mules in the pulling contest.

"How's it going?" Someone spoke at my elbow. They were leaning against the building.

"All right," I said. "How's it with you?"

"Hangin', ya know." He pushed from the wall with his hands slouched in his pockets, his shoulders hunched. He had that sightless cast in his eyes and deranged teeth.

Instantly I knew. A river rat.

"What's happenin'?" he said.

"Nothing."

"Yeh, I know whatcha mean." He was barefooted and his feet were wide flat things with splayed toes. One ankle was a dirty sore.

He edged closer. "You got a smoke?"

"No." He smelled bad but I didn't pull back.

"I run out."

"I don't smoke."

He leered. His body was curved in an ugly S with his scrawny neck bent forward. "I seen you come outta the drugstore 'while ago."

"So?"

"Purdy, ain't she?" Now he had little black rat's eyes. He was scratching his crotch with his hand in his pocket.

I felt my ears fill with blood.

"What happened to ya face?" He was still leering.

"Nothing." My teeth had clenched.

"I seen you got a knot on the back of ya head too."

"What's it to you?"

"Somebody must've hitcha a good un."

I turned to walk away and he grabbed my sleeve. "Hey, man, I'm jis' talkin'."

"Leave me alone." I jerked my arm away.

"Hail, man, I was jis' being friendly."

I stood my ground and we faced each other. Behind him now, sitting on the curb, I saw two others, and they were watching with a kind of moronic interest, but they were ready to help out. The one in front of me gestured with his head back toward them. "Them's my brothers." He spit on the sidewalk between us and winked. "You wanna start somethin', go ahead."

I would learn later his name was Spoon. The other two were Collard and Ham, and they were part of a big river rat family named Crane.

"I don't want to fight in the street," I said.

"Anywhere ya want to then. I don't care." He was still slouched, but his hands were out of his pockets.

"What did I do to you?" I didn't want to fight, but I didn't want to back down either.

He showed his rotten teeth. "You're new around here, ain'tcha?"

"I've been here before."

"Yeah? You must think you're somebody."

"I don't know what you're talking about."

"Then you better watch ya step or you're liable to end up with another knot on your head." He stuck his finger at my chest, and I knocked it away.

His eyes narrowed and his lips curled. "Sooo, ya wanna play."

"I don't want anything." I turned to go and his crabby claws grabbed my arm again.

I whirled and shoved him in the chest. He was all scrawny bones, no weight, and I easily jammed him back a couple of steps before he could catch himself.

Then he planted himself, but he didn't come back at me. Out of the corner of my eye I saw his two brothers getting up from the curb.

I turned again and started walking but I only got a few steps when I heard bare feet slapping the sidewalk, running up behind me. I ducked in time to catch him in midair, in the middle, and I lifted him with my shoulder and threw him down. He hit the cement hard on his hip and elbow and immediately started rolling in pain.

His brothers were coming and I didn't wait. I hurried across the street and down the block as fast as I could without actually running. Looking back once, I saw the one I'd thrown down was up and limping and the other two were helping. One woman was standing and looking, but that was all.

When I was far enough away, I slowed down and headed for the auction. If something had caused anything, I didn't know what it was, but there were people like that for no reason and you had to watch it. You could fight them and fight them and they'd still be there. They'd still be against you and coming. Even if you could get rid of them, others just like them would take their place. They'd breed and multiply in colonies, in nests and underground, and when they got too many, they'd swarm.

I could see the river rats in wave after wave coming out of the trees and overrunning the countryside.

If you can, Sailor said, you just stay out of their way. If you can't, and you gotta fight, you make sure you finish 'em.

69

3

The auction holding pen.

Horses and mules crowded together in one place don't show that much, not individually. They blur as a herd and what you see is a lumpy, moving layer on top, the restless hide of a single mass. That's what I was looking at. It was still not noon, time for the auction, and I was at the back pen checking the stock. Only a few other men were doing the same. Old trucks and horse trailers parked to the side. And, as yet, no Sailor.

I wasn't seeing much. Then, unexpectedly, two

heads in a far corner caught my eye. They were held higher than the others, and they had wide-set eyes and white noses.

I didn't have to look twice. "Hey!" I called. "Judy, Mawd!"

Their ears went up like spears and they craned their necks to find my voice. Then they saw me and started shoving through the crowd.

In another moment they were pushing their noses at me through the railing. I was massaging their faces and ears and they were nibbling my fingers with their rubbery lips. Ol' Judy and Mawd. We'd lived so close so long. It was really wonderful to breathe in their smells, the natural pungency of them, and to feel their hides and the big smooth life humming inside them. I could almost tell what they were thinking, and they didn't like it there. They weren't used to being crowded with other animals.

"Okay," I said, "lemme look atcha." I stepped back. There were some scratches, some mud in their hair, and their sides appeared a bit drawn, but they weren't hurt. They were fine.

I petted and fooled with them a while longer. Someone had brought them in to be sold. Someone had nabbed them wandering after the storm and figured to make a fast buck. "But not if I can help it," I said. "We'll get you home where you belong." Maybe I wouldn't be there, but Sailor would, and their home was with him too.

Good ol' Judy and Mawd. You had to know them. They were so particular and sensitive in so many ways, but when you respected that and treated them right, they'd do anything in the world for you. They liked their harnesses a certain way and their lines attached just so, and they had their places too, Judy on the right, Mawd left, and that's the way they had to be hitched, the way they insisted on being teamed, or they wouldn't go. It's the way they stood at rest, too, side by side. I could halt them and back them with a signal of my hand. With just my voice I could turn them on a dime completely around. I could make them stand. I could crawl between their legs, and they'd never move. They were so identical in their movements, in their size and strength, they might have been twins. Turned loose at night, they'd stroll together and act dreamy and nuzzle each other as if in love. But, naturally, being mules, that's as far as it went.

Now I needed to get them out of that place, and I talked to a man watering the stock, but he was no help.

"But they're mine," I said.

"I can't help it," he said. "Ya didn't bring 'em in. Ya wanna see 'bout 'em, you gotta talk to Sanders. He's the honcho."

Sanders, though, wouldn't be around until the auction started and that's when I decided I'd better get Sailor at Pauline's.

.   .   .

Her house was a big two-story affair behind an iron fence on the edge of town. Recently I've heard the place has been renovated and designated an historical building, but back then it was just a ramshackle house with a yard overgrown in stickery milkweed, and I'd never seen inside. So this was a first.

And first I remember the solid feel of the veranda underfoot. That meant the planking was seasoned hardwood and today when I again get the feel of solid support under some floor, my memory clicks back to

Pauline's. I get a vivid flash of me walking across that veranda without a face and my body is younger, it's somehow foreign, but the clothes are familiar, a gray shirt and denims, and I see my brogans feeling that floor and my hand is reaching out. The old-fashioned door is in front of me. It's an oval of glass with a frosted design around the edges and the glass is curtained inside.

I twisted the round bell in the middle of the door and heard the whirly jangly sound inside.

An old woman with a cleaning rag in her hand opened the door. The long hall behind her was dark, but I saw a clothes tree, a wall table, and curving stairs. The carpet was red. A round chandelier in the background framed her gray head.

She was looking at me with old eyes.

"I gotta see Sailor," I said.

"This is morning. Come back tonight."

"Well, it's kinda important. I gotta tell him something."

"Tell who?" Her hands were crippled and she rubbed them in her rag.

"Sailor."

"Sailor?"

"This is where he comes. He's probably sleeping."

"Oh, you're wanting to see *him*." She hobbled aside. "Well, come on in."

I stepped inside and she closed the door. "You wait here. I'll see if Pauline's awake yet."

"I just wanted to see Sailor."

"I know what you want. Now you just stay there till I get back." She went up the stairs, grunting, pulling at the handrail. Varicose globs showed through her black stockings.

The drapes were closed and the light was dim, but red fringe seemed to hang everywhere. A big room was off the hall, maybe the waiting room for customers. The red fringe hung from the lamp shades, the table covers, the chairs and footstools. All the furniture was brown heavy stuff and looked musty and comfortable.

While I waited, a door down the hall opened and a girl appeared. Maybe twenty feet away. She was wearing a ratty robe that stopped above her knees, and baggy wool socks that sagged around her ankles. No shoes. Her hair was tangled and there were dark circles under her eyes. She was looking at me, maybe trying to decide if I was a customer, if I was going to be worth anything. Then she turned back into her room and disappeared.

I'd find out later her name was Rita, and her robe, I remember thinking, needed to be longer. Her knees had been such knobby-looking things.

"Okay." The old woman came back down the stairs. "Pauline says you can go up. First door on the right, just go on in." She shuffled past me with her cleaning rag into the big room.

The first door on the right at the top of the stairs was slightly ajar, and I tapped.

"Yeah, come in." A throaty voice.

I think I was expecting something half forbidden, or languid and sensuous behind thin veils, maybe a naked woman spread-eagle—I was probably hoping to find everything.

But there was nothing to see. It was an ordinary bedroom and Pauline was under the covers, propped up on pillows, a little squinty from being awakened.

"You wanna see Sailor," she said.

"Yes, ma'am."

She had a nice face, almost a pretty face, but her hair was an orangy red.

"You know him?" She was quizzing me.

"Yes, I do."

"So you're a friend?" She shifted, a hefty, earthy body.

"Yes—I am." That body would feel soft and warm.

"Okay." I was being dismissed. "He's down the hall, last door." She turned away onto her side and the covers molded the shape of her hips, the curves and dips. Her hair was like a flame on the pillow. Then the rich aroma of her bed reached my nose.

The scent lifted me and I felt my body turning in air to leave. And turning, I noticed a bulletin board on the wall stuck with little business cards. Like in a Laundromat, I thought.

The last door opened into a small room without a window. Sailor was sprawled on a cot against the wall. Slobber from his mouth had made a wet place under his head, and he was breathing hard, gurgling in his throat. The muscles in his face had collapsed.

I couldn't rouse him. I pushed and pulled, but only one foot twitched, as if a spark had hit a gap it couldn't leap. His shoulders were spongy and disjointed. I shook him and tried sitting him up by the hair of his head, but his neck was limber and he fell back. It was about the worst I'd seen him. He smelled rotten.

I imagined his kidneys black as tar and his liver like cardboard, his blood only trickling in his veins.

The year before, we'd tried to sell blood. They'd pricked our fingers to take samples, and they tested the blood first by letting a drop fall through a vial of blue liquid, to see if the drop would stay solid going down.

And my blood sank like a beebee, but Sailor's sample went crazy. As soon as his drop hit the liquid, it shattered and sprinkled down through the blue like salt. He watched his blood fail, I think, without much interest and he wasn't bothered they wouldn't take his, but I got five dollars for a pint of mine.

I think I knew then he was dying but I couldn't imagine it. Not death. Not in Sailor. He'd always been too strong, his presence too solid, and I'd seen him come back too many times.

Like now, he was a sodden heap, his senses liquefied, his lungs filled with muck, but I'd seen that same junked body rise before, pull its strength together from out of nowhere, take a stance, and swing that ax again with the grace of an athlete, the power still in those long beautiful strokes, his rhythm still perfect, and I'd seen that happen too many times.

He'd come back this time too. The only problem was to get him up.

I went back to Pauline's door and tapped.

"Yeah, shit, what now?"

I tiptoed in. "I can't get him up."

"So? What'm I supposed to do?" Her head was half raised, and she was frowning.

"I need to tell him about our team. They got 'em at the auction."

"That's your problem." Back on her pillow. "I'm trying to sleep."

"But they're our mules, and they're going to auction 'em off." The covers outlined her breasts.

"Honey, I don't know nothing about mules." She shifted and a fascinating slice of her thigh showed.

I became stupid. I heard myself saying, "Well, they're smarter than horses."

She looked at me with one eyebrow raising and I kept going. "They are. A horse'll eat poisoned sorghum, but a mule knows better, and a horse'll eat till he founders, but a mule won't."

"What're you talking about?"

"You said you didn't know about mules."

"And I ain't interested neither."

"But did you know a mule can also go longer without water?"

"Hey." She stopped me and bared her teeth. "I'm through being nice, understand?"

"I'm sorry."

"I'm tired. I got to get some sleep. I've been on my back all night."

"I guess you work pretty hard." That slipped out without thinking. I meant to sympathize probably. I wasn't trying to be smart. But I knew I shouldn't have said it.

Her eyes narrowed.

Then a strange thing happened. Her lips slowly widened into a smile and she laughed, a nice big laugh full of humor.

I felt embarrassed. More of her thigh was showing, and she didn't care. "I'm sorry," I said.

"Naw, you're all right, you're funny. What's your name?"

"Bud." I couldn't quite look at her. "Well, it's really Bobby, but that's what I'm called."

"What's Sailor—your dad?"

I hesitated. "I guess."

She smiled again, but this time her eyes softened and she asked kindly, "You got a problem with Sailor?"

"Well, he's passed out and I need to tell him about our team before they get auctioned off."

"That old mule team?"

"Well, they're not just old mules. Mules are—"

She cut in. "Yeah, I know, mules are smarter'n horses. I don't need to hear it again—Okay, shit, let's see what we can do."

She threw the covers back and I saw her completely naked. She swung her legs wide and got out of bed, a really inspiring sight. Her hair was orangy down there too, and her body was big and hefty but beautifully curved. Her thighs were fat and dimpled and nice and round. Her breasts looked wonderfully full and upright. There were sexy dips in her hips and a pout in her navel, a real woman's body. She was warm smelling from the bed and moved saucily, carelessly.

I took it all in with my eyes wide open.

She put on a red gauzy gown that still showed everything, only better somehow, and gave me a look. "C'mon," she said, "let's get him up."

I followed the outline of her churning hips.

Sailor was the same as I'd left him.

"Jesus," Pauline said, "you'd think I was running a fuckin' flophouse."

She jerked Sailor to a sitting position and started slapping him. His eyes rolled back in his head. And she punched him and hit his ribs and slapped him again. I hated to watch it but he started coming around. He started babbling, "Okay, okay, okay—"

We got him to his feet, and he was still out of it, barely able to stand, but between us we staggered him down the stairs and into the kitchen. All the way he was making sounds: "Yuh, 'kay, okay, yuh, okay—"

We stuck his head under the faucet in the sink and ran cold water, and he began to hold his legs better, but he was still a soggy and limp body when we sat him down at the table and Pauline gave him coffee. His eyes were nowhere, and he had to hold the cup in both hands to get it to his mouth. His face was gray. Only the colors in his tattoos were heightened. They were vivid reds and blues, the brightest I'd seen.

"Okay, you got him now." Pauline was leaving. "See if you can get three or four cups down him. There's plenty in the pot." She regarded Sailor a moment. "Why does he do that, you know?"

"I dunno, he just does."

"He's killing hisself, you know that?"

"Well, he does what he wants." Sailor was hearing but probably not understanding. His mouth was mushed over his cup and his eyes were glittering in their sockets.

"He wants to kill hisself, he oughta just go ahead put a bullet through his head." She looked disgusted.

"He'll be all right. He gets like this and then he bounces back."

She lowered her voice to me. "You and him get along?"

"I guess—I don't like the way we live, though."

She nodded. I couldn't keep my eyes off the outline of her body. The brown circles around her nipples stood out.

"Okay," she said, "I'm going to sleep and I don't wanna be bothered. I don't care if he drops dead—okay?"

"Okay." I also meant thank you.

The light showed between her legs as she walked out.

The old kitchen was large and homey and the big windows were full of sunshine. It was a place where the

7 9

whores could eat, I supposed, and not have to be seen in town. There was the smell of bread and baloney somewhere. A black cat was sitting on top of the refrigerator, slowly waving its tail.

Sailor drank his coffee on his own. I didn't have to make him. He had to force himself, you could tell—an old act of will—but he sipped steadily, and gradually he was able to hold himself straighter. His eyes began to focus more, and after three cups he knew where he was. His hands were still trembling but his face was lifting. He stood to test himself, wobbled a little, and sat back down.

I poured his fourth cup of coffee while he put his elbows on the table and held his head. We had yet to speak.

Then he looked up. "So what's your problem?"

"I don't have one. I thought you did."

"What're you doing here?"

I told him about Judy and Mawd.

"That's good," he said. "You found 'em, that's good." The clear way he pronounced his words was out of all proportion to the way he looked. But he was like that. He could make his brain come back before his body was ready for it. He coughed up a glob of matter and swallowed it back.

He said vacantly, "Mules—" He was staring at a world in his cup. The lines in his face were hard and deep. They were bad weather lines and battle lines. His mind had dug trenches in his face.

"Mules," he repeated. "You know, it's funny. A mule's born, he founds a new race. The whole race is him. Then he dies and the race goes with him. He can't pass one part of himself on, not one hair, and he's looked down on 'cause he's not a horse— So while he's here, he's got to have something, and he does. He's got forbearance. That's what he's got, and he knows that's all there is." He raised his eyes to me. "Funny, ain't it?"

"I guess." I couldn't match his eyes. They were asking for something I didn't have. Some kind of crazy understanding maybe. Or agreement. I didn't know. When he set his eyes like that, I'd look away.

Sailor was always talking, saying something was nothing and nothing was something, saying there's no wealth but life and you gotta have understanding apart from words, and something either happens or it doesn't and all those things. Nothing that made any sense or that I wanted to hear. And I'd let it go.

I think now there was probably some kind of philosopher inside Sailor trying to get out, but I couldn't see it then. It was just Sailor talking.

"We better go," I said. "The auction's starting."

Sailor closed his eyes and sat back. "Yeah, okay, in about another minute." He was trying to take some deep breaths through his nose.

The old cleaning woman came in, sweeping the floor. She paid us no attention and worked in silence. The rag was stuffed in her apron. Holes were cut in her slippers for her bunions and her crippled hands seemed barely able to grasp the broom handle but she moved at a steady pace. When she came to our table, she said, "Lift your feet." We did. She swept under them, picked up the dirt in a dust pan, and went away.

"That was Stella," Sailor said. "When she was young, she worked the mining towns in Colorado. Probably made a million dollars—now look at her."

Poor old woman, I thought.

Sailor went on. "Yeah, her problem was she got old. And the demand for old whores is kinda slack."

"C'mon, Sailor, we gotta go." I was afraid he was forgetting.

"Okay." He gathered himself to stand. Then he stood and wavered. "Just a second." He looked suddenly sicker, but he fought it and steadied, found his better legs and cleared the air with his hands. "One thing," he said.

He walked to the refrigerator, took out a jar of pickles and started drinking the juice.

"This helps," he said.

At that moment the girl in the ratty robe walked in and passed between us. She appeared to skate the floor in her baggy socks to the cupboard and took out a glass. As she turned, she saw what Sailor was drinking and stopped.

Sailor grinned and raised his jar to her. "Cheers."

She looked at him dully, without expression, then walked out of the kitchen with her glass pressed to her chest. Her hair was still messy, and there still were circles under her eyes, but this time I saw that if she made herself up, she might be pretty.

"Rita," Sailor said, "funny gal."

"Sailor—"

"Yeh—yeh, I'm ready." He gulped the last of the pickle juice and wiped his mouth with the back of his hand.

We'd get Judy and Mawd, we'd do that first, then I'd tell him I was leaving.

We were walking the dump truck road that cut the corner of town, the shortest way. Sailor was a little gray in the open air but feeling better and getting stronger by the minute.

Orangy things were on my mind.

"How much they charge?" I asked.

A small glance at me. "Whataya wanna know for?"

"Just asking."

We kept walking.

Finally he said, "A quickie's ten dollars."

"What's a quickie?"

"Just what it says. They get you in and out as quick as they can."

I figured in my head. Ten dollars—seven hamburgers, five movies.

"What's another price?" I asked.

"All night's fifty."

"And what do you get for all night?"

"A little more conversation."

I figured the cost of that too.

Then I decided, for fifty dollars I'd probably rather just talk to myself.

We stopped to check on Judy and Mawd. They were still in the holding pen and still okay, so we went on inside the sale barn and sat in the bleachers with the rest of the people. A couple hundred maybe in the crowd around us.

I wasn't sure how Sailor was going to handle the situation. He'd do things different ways according to how he felt. Sometimes he'd be surprisingly easy, almost gentle. He'd get a problem straightened out and leave everybody feeling good. Other times, he'd chop people down like he was wading through trees with an ax.

I don't think he planned.

The auctioneer's chant was coming over the loudspeakers. Bidding was going on, and the action was fast. A head would barely nod somewhere, a man would blink an eye, flick a finger, give some invisible indication, and the two spotters on the stand would pick it up and relay it. They'd catch another sign instantly, and the auctioneer would build to the next level without missing a beat. The bids were caught and layered in the air with the stuttering pudding of his voice. It was a wonderful thing to see, and I didn't know how anybody kept up.

One horse caused considerable interest, a beautiful roan gelding. Some man rode it around the ring to show how it handled, and the crowd rippled. It was a sleek, high-stepping animal, and the bids came fast and heavy from all over. Then it narrowed down to two men on opposite sides of the stands. They kept topping each other, and the auctioneer's head kept going back and forth. Finally one man gave up and stopped. The other man had bid over two thousand dollars with a blank face, and the big gelding, before being ridden out, reared and pawed in the air.

After that they auctioned off five or six more animals.

Then Judy and Mawd were brought in.

"Now here's a good strong team," the auctioneer began, "a fine matched pair—"

Judy and Mawd were being led around the ring and they looked good. Their ears were alert and they held their heads high. Their narrow hooves stepped daintily in the soft dirt and you could see the way their muscles moved. I felt proud.

"Now what'm I bid? Do I hear—"

"Hold it!" Sailor's voice overruled the loudspeakers. "Hold it right there!" He stood up beside me, and heads turned to look. "That's stolen property!"

The crowd all at once was quiet. The auctioneer was stopped.

I felt suddenly exposed. Then Sailor was making his way down the bleachers, people were leaning aside, and I had to hurry to follow.

We climbed the fence down into the ring, crossed it, and climbed up the other side in front of the auctioneer's table. The name Sanders was stitched on the man's shirt, and the two spotters had closed with him.

"That's my team," Sailor said. "Somebody stole 'em."

Sanders looked at some papers in his hand until he found a name. "Oh, shit," he said. He raised his eyebrows, showed the name to his two spotters, and they looked at each other knowingly.

"The Cranes," Sanders said, the name of the people who'd brought Judy and Mawd in for auction.

"I don't care who they are," Sailor said. "They're trying to get away with my property."

Sanders put his hand over his microphone. "You can prove that team's yours now?"

"Anybody at the sawmill knows 'em. Chubb, Gore, the rest. They all know they're mine. Hell, you've seen me driving 'em."

Sanders looked down in the ring. "Yeah, I guess I have, pulling your wagon." He pulled at his ear and thought. "Okay, I'll get 'em up here—if that's what you want?"

"Get 'em up here." Sailor was standing hard, his feet spread.

Sanders looked nervous. "But no trouble up here. Just take it easy. We'll get it straight." He took a breath and spoke into his microphone. "Spoon, Collard, Ham Crane—come to the stand, please." The announcement caused a small commotion in the crowd.

Then I saw them, and my stomach tightened. They were coming from the back of the barn and taking their time. As they progressed through the crowd, a rustle of murmuring rose behind them.

It was the three I'd run into earlier on the street. Of course. They lived back in the woods along the river not that far from our camp. After the storm they would've been the first to find Judy and Mawd.

Spoon was the one I'd thrown on the sidewalk, and he was leading the way. His lips were sneering. His two brothers, Collard and Ham, were right behind him, aping his movements. Their eyes were vacant dead spots in their heads and their mouths were hanging open, showing their tongues.

The lump on my head started throbbing.

Then I noticed an astounding thing. They'd been singled out, called to the front, and everybody was looking. They were a spectacle. I might've tried to crawl in a hole. But they were enjoying being the show, you could tell. They were almost strutting, grinning idiotically. It didn't matter what people thought. To them it was attention and they were lapping it up. They were twisting their asses, making sure the crowd got a good look.

Sailor had fixed his eyes on them as they came, and I could feel a slow burn starting inside him. He was drawing in his mind that old line they'd better not step over.

Then they were there, and we were all in front of Sanders' table.

Spoon gave me a hard look and turned to Sanders. "Yuh, what?"

Sanders raised his chin. "Those two mules down there, they yours?"

"I reckon. We brung 'em, didn't we?"

"Where'd you get 'em?"

"Whataya mean? We own 'em. Don't we?" He turned to his brothers, and they nodded stupidly, automatically.

"I need to know where you got 'em."

"Hail, we bought 'em. I got the papers right here." He fished in his back pocket for a scrap of paper and handed it to Sanders.

Sailor shifted his weight and held tight.

Sanders read the paper and passed it to Sailor. From the side I saw "bil of sale" written across the top, and then some scribbly handwriting and a signature I couldn't decipher. The paper had been torn from some lined tablet.

Sanders was talking. "That says you bought two mules for a hundred dollars from somebody named Murdock. Who's Murdock?"

"I dunno." Spoon spit between his feet. "We run into him up the road a ways, said he was from Mason County, that's what he told us."

"Well, a hundred dollars for two good mules, that doesn't seem like much."

"We got us a bargain. Hail, the man said he needed the money, said he'd take anything he could get."

"And you didn't give him a check. You paid him in cash, of course?"

"'Course. Hail, who's gonna trust a bank? Shit." He grinned obnoxiously.

Sailor had waited long enough. He tore the paper in half and tossed it in Spoon's face. "You're a damned liar."

Spoon didn't blink. "The hail I am. I bought them mules, I jis' proved it."

"You didn't prove nothing."

Sanders leaned across the table and put his arm between them. "Now, hold it, just calm down."

"He called me a liar. He tore up my bill of sale." Spoon was acting abused and hurt.

"I said hold it a second. We got a dispute here." Sanders kept his arm out. "What you need to do is settle this someplace else."

"But I brung 'em in to sell," Spoon said.

"Well, you can't do that now."

"You want to," Sailor said, "we can call in the sheriff."

Spoon blinked. "Whataya mean?"

"Look, I'm not going to argue," Sanders said. "Those mules belong to this man here. He's got people to back him up on that."

"And I got my proof too." Spoon snatched up a piece of his torn paper. "I got the bill of sale right here."

Sanders shook his head. "What you need to do is find the man you got 'em from, that Murdock fella, if that's where you got 'em, and take it up with him. They weren't his to sell either."

"Whataya mean?" Spoon was obviously playing it dumb all the way.

But Sailor had had enough, "This is bullshit." He turned to Sanders. "What's the verdict?"

"I don't take responsibility." Sanders waved to the man in the ring to take Judy and Mawd back to the pen. "The mules go back outside. You two can do what you want to with 'em out there."

"That suits me." Sailor was being reasonable.

But Spoon glared at Sanders. "You mean you ain't gonna auction 'em?"

"They're not yours to sell, Spoon." Sanders was trying to be patient. "Besides, who'd bid on 'em now?"

"So you're jis' gonna let him take 'em away from me?" Spoon's mouth was turning mean.

Sanders braced. "Now let's get this straight. I don't take responsibility. I don't care who owns those mules. But I can't sell anything where the ownership's in question right up front—you got that? And don't you try coming back on me either. You got an argument, it's with this man, not me." Sanders folded his papers.

Spoon turned to Sailor now. "Yeah, that's right. My problem's with you, ain't it?" He was sneering again.

Sailor shrugged. "I tell you what, let's just call in the sheriff."

"Shee-it!" Spoon spit and looked at his brothers. "I don't need no law to hold my hand."

"Then any way you want to." Sailor was ready, and I was afraid it was going to start right there. There was a tension in the crowd and I could feel the eyes watching.

"Yeah, well, you take them mules, you'll see."

"Any time." Sailor waited.

"C'mon." I nudged Sailor's elbow. "Let's go."

Spoon abruptly turned on me. "And you better watch it too. I know you."

"C'mon," I repeated.

Sailor said to Spoon, "You know something, you're a fuckin' idiot, a complete stupid fuckin' idiot."

"I know my rights."

"That's enough now." Sanders' arm was out again. "Take it outside, I mean it, not in here."

"C'mon, Sailor, let's just go." I pulled his arm.

Sailor held another moment, then turned. "Yeh, c'mon, this is stupid."

We were moving to leave when Spoon let go. "Yeah, tuck your tail and run. You call me a liar and you're another one, you're a—" That's as far as he got.

Sailor whirled, and the next thing I saw, Spoon was whacked backwards into his two brothers, and all three were crumpling to the floor. Sailor had caught Spoon in the face with the back of his fist. He'd swung his arm around like a baseball bat, and a splatter of blood was still flying in the air. A tooth was slowly tumbling in the splatter. I heard the small cracking sound of bone, and above that the harder sound of the blow was rebounding from the bleachers.

Sanders and the spotters were immediately in between. The three Cranes scrambled to their feet, and they didn't jump up to fight, but neither did they back away. Spoon was holding his face with his hands, and Collard and Ham were helping. Sailor was simply standing his ground.

"That's enough, enough," Sanders was saying.

But he didn't have to worry. That's all there was. The only problem was, it had happened in front of everybody. I can see that now. The crowd was humming.

The spotters were trying to get us to leave in separate directions, and finally we did. The Cranes, clutched and sulking together, made their way to the side exit, and Sailor and I walked out the back.

I looked back once. Spoon's face was an ugly splotch of dripping red. His nose was flat, and his eyes were full of hate. He was looking at me, though, not at Sailor, and that was a surprise.

Then we were outside, and it was over, and I was trying to feel relieved.

Sailor was rubbing his fist and making a face. "Damn, outta joint," he said. He stuck his hand out to me. "Here, pull on it, pull 'er back in before it gets too swollen."

The third knuckle on his left hand was crooked and humped up.

"Do it," he said.

I didn't exactly want to, but I held his wrist while he braced his shoulder. Then I grabbed his finger and yanked. There was weird pop and I felt my knees react, but Sailor only took his hand back and tested his grip. "That got it," he said. "That's good."

In another breath he said, "Fuckin' river rats, oughta all be drowned."

"I don't think they're finished either," I said.

"They are for now."

We walked on to the pen, where Judy and Mawd had been returned, and they were standing near the rail waiting for us. Their big eyes were liquid and shining.

"What about later?" I said.

"What's later comes later."

"There's a bunch of 'em, though."

"They need a bunch."

"But what if a lot of 'em come—"

"Bud—" He stopped me. "You keep worrying, you're going to turn gray-headed."

We borrowed a couple of ropes from one of the stockmen and led Judy and Mawd away. Sailor wanted to let them graze in a pasture near the fair grounds, where there was also a nice little stream. That's where we usually staked them in town and it was all right with whoever owned the property.

After that we were sitting in the City Cafe. Sailor wanted a bowl of chili. He needed the grease for his stomach, he said, and I ordered a hamburger and French fries.

I was probably being too quiet, trying to think of the right way to tell him.

"Okay, let's have it," he said.

"What?"

"What's on your mind."

"Whataya mean?"

"You got something you wanna say, let's hear it."

"I don't have anything."

He shrugged. "Suit yourself."

Our food came. There was a good after-lunch crowd, and the waitress was trying to be fast, but she was behind serving extra butter and refills. Sailor had to stop her to ask for the catsup, and that made her look even more harassed.

There were too many pickles in my hamburger when it came and I picked them out and put them on the side of my plate. I also liked mayonnaise instead of mustard, but I'd forgotten to say that.

Sailor crumbled his crackers and dusted his palms. Then he blew on his spoon to cool it.

"I'm leaving," I said.

"Oh, yeh?" He was blowing on his chili. "Where to?"

"I'm going to stay here in town." My fries were long and golden and I sprinkled them with salt.

"What're you gonna do?"

"I dunno, get me a job, find me a room somewhere."

He took a bite, and then another, not bothering to look up.

Then he asked, "Tell me something—where'd you get that bump on your head?"

"Somebody threw a rock."

He looked at me now. "And what?"

"Nothing. I didn't see who did it. It was dark." I was talking easily enough.

"You weren't asking for it then?"

"Nope." I bit into my hamburger. "I was just walking along minding my own business. I don't know why it happened." The shadow had darted in the darkness, in the alley, and I had grabbed the dead limb that was too brittle and light. I was remembering that.

Sailor crumbled another cracker. "So you think you're ready?"

"I've been ready for a long time."

He nodded. "I figured you'd been thinking that."

"Well, I guess I have."

We ate for a while in silence. The people in the café seemed to be moving through space, and they were silent too. But I knew that was only an impression.

Sailor was into his bowl. "Good chili. How's your hamburger?"

"Pretty good."

He wiped his mouth with his hand and sat back. "What kind of job you gonna get?"

"I dunno. I might try at the sawmill."

"They pay minimum, you know that."

"I don't care."

"They make everybody line up and punch a time clock."

"It'd be a job, though."

"Yeah—" He scratched at his chest, at the hairs sticking out of his shirt. "Well, I guess you gotta learn."

"I can take care of myself."

He grinned. "Yeh, you probably can. You got a good head on your shoulders when you wanna use it. 'Course, a lot of times you let your feelings get in the way and you don't think at all."

"I can think when I want to."

"And you can probably hold your own too, I guess. In most cases. Unless you happen to run into a stacked deck."

"I can handle a stacked deck too."

"Oh, you reckon?"

"I know what I can do. You're not going to change my mind." I'd finished about half my hamburger, but I didn't want the rest. Not now.

"What are you now, twelve, thirteen?"

"Whataya mean twelve?" I knew he didn't keep up with dates, but that was some kind of insult. "I'm fourteen."

"Naw, you're not fourteen."

"Oh, yeah? Next month, I am."

He was puzzled. He thought. Then he said, "Yeh, I guess you are. It's been about ten years now, a little more."

Ten years since he'd come from the sea and taken me away to live in the trees, out there, here and yonder and nowhere. He was counting as if the time had passed him by, but I'd already counted the summers that never changed and my days and nights alone. I'd marked that time.

"You know," he said, "you're a little ahead of me. I was fifteen before I was on my own."

He let it hang and I waited.

"I started out hitchhiking," he said. "One place I got to was San Diego. First time I ever saw the ocean and I just stood there looking at it. There was a destroyer anchored out in the harbor and I can remember thinking it looked just like it was cut out of cardboard, right off a cereal box." He was looking at his hands, remembering. "Then I got on up to San Francisco, and I walked out to the middle of the Golden Gate Bridge and looked down at the water. It looked about a hundred miles down—I wondered what it would be like to jump off. It was night and there was the reflection of a full moon on the water." His eyes were lost. "It was real pretty."

"But you didn't jump," I said.

That brought him out of it. "No—I didn't. But I think I came pretty close."

"You wanted to?"

"Oh, I dunno. You know, in those days, why not?"

"That's sorta the way I see things now."

"Yeh, I know you do."

Our eyes met, his were sad, and I looked away. "I've made up my mind," I said. "You're not going to talk me out of it."

"I'm not trying to." He shifted his seat and his mood changed that quick. "Hell, when've I ever told you what to do?"

"Lots of times."

"When you're bothering me, to get you out of my hair, but when've I ever stopped you from doing anything you wanted to?"

"I never wanted to live in the trees."

"You never had to."

"But that's where we've been, that's where you made us live."

"But you didn't have to—hell, you could've run off anytime. I didn't have you locked up, did I?"

That caught me. I opened my mouth and shut it. And then just stared at him. It was the truth, I'd never been locked up. But still—

"I should've left before," I said. "You probably wanted me to."

He looked down and stirred at his chili. "No—I never wanted you to do that."

"You acted like it."

"You might've taken me wrong too."

"If I had a choice, you should've told me."

"I tell you things, you don't listen." He looked around for the waitress. "How 'bout some coffee?"

"I'm leaving."

"How 'bout some pie?"

"I don't want anything." I felt I had shorted myself somehow. I'd had a choice and didn't know it. I'd felt caged but the cage door had been open the whole time. At the same time I knew I'd never been ready till now.

Sailor got his coffee and started sipping it. "How much money you got?"

"Fifty dollars."

"Think that'll do you?"

"I can make it last."

"I can let you have some—"

I shook my head.

Sailor ran his finger around the edge of his cup. "You know, there's some things I never told you, never got around to, I guess."

"Like what?"

"Oh, I dunno. About myself, when you were born, things like that."

His voice sounded different and I waited.

"I oughta tell you sometime," he said.

"Go ahead." I was curious about a lot of things. My mother was wearing turquoise and riding a spotted pony through the clouds, and her dark hair was flying— Or maybe not.

"Well, this might not be the time."

"But you can tell me something."

He rested his elbows on the table and clasped both hands around his cup. "One thing, I want you to know this, I'm proud of the way you studied your books. That's gonna hold you up one of these days. You won't be sorry."

"Is that what you wanted to tell me? Is that all?" I felt disappointed.

"I guess I was leading up to saying that's the way I did it too. I never went to school much either. I educated myself. And there was a time I read everything I could get my hands on. I wanted to know everything." The corners of his mouth tried to smile. "You didn't know that about me, did you?"

I didn't care either.

"What about my mother?" I said.

His eyes dropped. "Your mother—" A pause. Then, "She was pretty, Bud. Very pretty."

"What happened?"

"She died when you were born—I wasn't there."

"But what happened?"

"We had a problem." He was looking at his hands. "Her family didn't like me. They didn't want her to come with me. And when she did, they quit having anything to do with her. Well, her mother did, but her mother didn't have much say. They closed her out. And then, I dunno, I felt sorta cooped up, and I was out running around—" He waved his hand. "I've never talked about it."

"So you left her?"

"No—I just wasn't around. The Claytons had to take you in."

"Murph and Mattie."

He nodded. "They were good people."

"Then why'd you come back for me?"

"I dunno, it started bothering me." He shook his head. "I figured I owed you."

I felt stunned. "Owed me?" I'd been living good with those people. I had a bed, a dog, fried apple pies. I'd been happy. "So you thought taking me to live in the trees was paying me back? You thought living out away from people and never seeing anybody was doing me a favor?"

His face darkened quickly and tightened. "You grew up healthy, didn't you? When were you ever sick a day?"

"I never had anybody to play with. I never had any friends."

"You learned to take care of yourself."

"I wanted to be around people and live in town."

"You got to grow up naturally. You didn't have to be like everybody else."

"That's what I want, though. I don't want to be different. I want to be like everybody else, dammit!"

He looked at me as if for the first time.

"You didn't have to owe me," I said. "You didn't do me any favor."

He wagged his head.

My face was hot. "I guess you think I owe you something now?"

"Not a thing." His eyes were hard, black. "Why should you? You worked, paid your way— Look, you didn't have a choice with me, okay? Well, I didn't have a choice with you either, so we're even." He turned away.

Again we had another one of our silences, a strangeness suddenly between us. It always happened when we argued. He'd pull up, shut a door, and we'd be closed off from each other.

But I didn't want to part on a bad note. When he opened the door again, I wanted to be able to say something we both could feel good about.

But what? Sailor—we had some good times, didn't we? Fishing. Remember when we caught that big bass, that must've weighed ten pounds. It was on my line, but you had to help haul it in, and we were laughing and yelling, it was so big. That was a time. And the squirrels at that one camp, that used to come up and eat out of our hands. They'd eat breakfast with us and we named them after the trees, Piney, Oaky, Scrub— Remember how we used to lie back at night and watch the stars fall? One night there must've been a thousand. They were like a shower across half the sky. And we'd build waterwheels. We had one going in every stream we ever camped near. And the gardens we planted. Watching 'em grow. The radishes and tomatoes, beans and all. We had some good things to eat. And the time the raccoons got our corn. They stripped the rows one night like a threshing machine. And the carnival that time—you broke the hammer and I won a stuffed tiger. What ever happened to that stuffed tiger? We had some good times, didn't we?

Sailor turned. "You know—" He rubbed his chin and his whiskers were raspy. "There's gonna be a pulling contest this weekend, at the fair."

"I know, I've been looking at the posters."

"You want to, we could enter it. We got Judy and Mawd back, we could win it." He was playing with his cup.

I could see the crowd cheering, the flags waving from the tent tops. "But you don't need me," I said.

"Yeh, I do. The rules call for a driver and a helper, to line the team straight, to save time."

"I'm leaving, though."

"I'm not trying to stop you. You don't wanna be a helper, I'll find somebody else." He sat back.

I wanted to be in the contest but in my mind I'd already left and I didn't want to backtrack. "I guess I could meet you at the time," I said.

"That's fine. But I can count on you?"

"That's this Saturday?"

"That's right. There'll be some betting going on too. You can chance that fifty you got, maybe turn it into a hundred."

"I don't know about that."

"You could win yourself a little extra to go on."

"Yeh, but I dunno." I'd saved that fifty as a nest egg and Sailor knew I didn't like chances.

He let it go. "Well, the time comes, I'll be placing some bets, you can let me know. Now, what about your clothes, your extra duds and bedroll?"

They were back at camp. I'd forgotten them.

"I'm going back tomorrow," Sailor said. "You want me to, I'll bring 'em in for you Friday night."

The contest. My clothes. There were still ties. But

it wouldn't be for long. "Yeh, you can bring 'em in," I said.

"Anything else?"

"I guess not."

"Then that about wraps it up."

Once again we sat. And I felt funny. What was I doing?

"I'm glad we can part on good terms," I said.

"Sure. Nothing to be mad at, is there?"

I tried to smile. "We had some good times, didn't we?"

"Wasn't all bad, was it? Overall, I'd say we made a pretty good team. We could lay down that timber when we wanted to, couldn't we?"

"You did the big part."

"But you held your own too. You knew what your job was and went after it. I didn't have to tell you."

"I didn't like working cedar, though."

"Rough stuff. I didn't much like it myself."

"Hardwood wasn't that easy either."

"But most of the time we had the firs and pine. We could lay that down pretty good."

"Yeah, we could. We did." I could see those tall trees slowly falling, their tops coming down, crashing down. Then me walking them, stripping the branches until they were smooth rolls of timber. We'd work under them with the chains and hitch Judy and Mawd and drag those rolls out for loading, one after another. Over the years we'd chopped down whole forests the sawmills had turned into trainloads of red and yellow lumber. Looking back, you'd think we might have been an army, we'd cut down so much. And never with a saw. Only axes.

At the same time, we hadn't made a dent. Sailor

said. You cut a track and the trees grow back right be-hind you, in twenty years or whenever, it makes no dif-ference, you look around and you can't even tell where you've been.

"Anyway," Sailor said, "we'll probably see each other around. I'm gonna be out there on that tract for a couple more months. You're going to be here in town. We'll probably run into each other a couple times any-way. And we got that contest this weekend."

"That's right." I was going to look forward to that.

We were scooting our chairs to leave. I knew he'd be going to Dominoes again and then to Pauline's maybe that night. I had to see about a room and meet Hominy down by the river.

"While I'm thinking about it," he said, "one thing." We both stopped scooting our chairs. "Some advice." He half grinned. "That is, if you'll take a little advice?"

"Sure." Why not?

"One of these days, you're gonna find things pull-ing at you. Everybody does. You're gonna be in a spot and not know which way to turn. That happens, trust yourself."

I waited for more, but that was it.

And he repeated it, "Just remember that. Trust yourself."

It seemed simple enough.

. . .

I asked at the Belvedere and Lew said he could give me a weekly rate, fifteen dollars for the last room on the bottom floor. It was smaller, an old utility room, and there was no window, but I took it.

He said I could wait to pay until I found a job and

I accepted that. He also gave me a key to the back door, which was handier, and I felt satisfied I'd taken care of my first step—a regular place in town to live.

Lew could pussyfoot up and down the hall all he wanted, I could lock my door inside. He could make his tacky little sounds on the linoleum all night and it wouldn't bother me. He was so little and frail anyway.

Just the same, I told him, "Now, let's get this straight. I don't want you sneaking up on me every-where—you got that?"

"Oh, no!" he said. "I mean, I won't."

He was so damned silly reacting, nervous and happy at the same time, I decided, at heart he was probably a good enough person. He just had a hard time finding anybody who could stand him.

And since I still had time in the afternoon before meeting Hominy, I went on to see about a job.

I was walking to the sawmill about a mile west of town and feeling good. The parting with Sailor had been friendly. I'd gotten a room at a good rate just like that. I was going to meet a girl down by the river and the pulling contest would be a big event. It was all coming up. Dallas, it seemed, was just beyond those small hills, and I'd soon be on my way. I could feel my face blooming and I heard somebody walking in my shoes whistling.

Then I heard the whine of the saws in the air and in the distance the separate structures of the sawmill stood clear. I'd been there before so I knew what they were, but this time they looked different. It might have been the light or the shading from the clouds, I don't know. This time the whole place looked flimsy. The stacks of lumber, the kiln, the sheds and office were all wooden and appeared distinctly makeshift. Definitely impermanent. All that wood could burn up or blow away in a wind. The mounds of sawdust would smolder longer but they would disappear too.

It was a curious thing. I had never before thought of a workplace as a passing thing. But there it was. That sawmill could shut down and turn into a ghost town. It could fall to pieces and rot in the rain. You could blink your eyes and it would be gone.

I thought, for the first time, the place you work comes and goes. Where you build is shifting sand.

Chubb was a beefy man with a sunburned face and he was the foreman, I guess, or the manager. Anyway, I knew he ran the place, and I found him back with a truck, unloading timber.

I asked him if he was hiring.

"Well, not right now," he said. "We're pretty well caught up." Then he gave me a slanting look with Oriental eyes, slits in his round face. "I thought you were working with Sailor."

"I'm on my own now."

"Zat right? How old are you?"

"Sixteen." That was the first time I lied about my age, but for the next five years I'd always be two years older.

He shook his head. He had a clipboard in his hands and pretended to check something.

A man on the truck was having trouble with the last boom that cinched a chain around the logs. He had loosened the others, but this one wasn't giving.

"I can do that," I said. I meant I could free the boom.

The man was cussing with the boom, "Goddamned, cocksuckin', muthafuckin' sonofabitch!'' The boom was frozen.

"I could give him a hand," I said.

Chubb gestured. "All right, hell, give him a hand."

I climbed to the top of the five rolls of timber. The man pried with a crowbar and I swung the sledgehammer and the boom popped free. I could swing a sledge the same as an ax.

Chubb had watched, and when I climbed down he said, "You wanna work, I'll tell you what—you can fill out an application. Maybe we'll have something coming up. You can keep checking back with me."

We went to the office and I filled in the application form. I wrote the best I could and made sure I didn't miss any blanks.

Chubb looked at the finished form and again shook his head. "You know something, ordinarily I wouldn't hire anybody that had this kind of application."

I was taken back. "What's wrong?"

"You write too good. That's how I judge a man, on his application. If he can't spell and I can't read his writing, I hire him 'cause that means he's dumb enough to work here. Somebody writes like this"—he lifted my form—"they're too smart to stick around."

"I want to work, though. I need a job."

"Well, I'll make an exception. I know the kind of work you've been doing. And who knows?" He patted my shoulder. "You might just turn out dumb enough after all."

He walked me outside. "You check back with me."

"I will. I appreciate it."

"But just as long as you don't start fights."

"I don't."

"Well, I was noticing your face—"

"I got struck by lightning."

"Zat right?" He appeared interested. "I knew a fella once that was struck by lightning. Magnetized his right hand, that's a fact. He could pick up nails with the ends of his fingers."

"That didn't happen to me."

"He was a mechanic down in Olney, and he finally had to quit his job. He'd pick up a wrench and it'd stick to his hand and he couldn't get rid of it. Nearly drove his wife crazy too, supposedly." He grinned with his Oriental eyes. "When they crawled in bed, she never knew what he was liable to have still stuck to his fingers down there."

"I'll check back with you," I said.

He waved. "Yeh, you do that."

On the way to the river, an old junky pickup slowed down to cross a road ahead of me. It had clappy sideboards and chicken wire around the back, and I didn't see Spoon, but Collard was driving and Ham was sitting beside him.

They had slowed down to let me know they were watching me, then pulled away. Their engine was misfiring and left behind little coughing puffs of black smoke.

When I got to the road, though, and looked in the direction they had driven, they were nowhere to be seen.

4

We were on a raft and the river was high and running hard. There was a rough and muddy look down the middle. Sailor knew I couldn't swim but we were crossing to the other side and he was using a pole and pushing us. Then the river appeared to well and widen. "We better turn back," I said. The raft had no center and yawed and I had no place to hold. Sailor was poling us into the deep where the water was heavy and the raft was weightless. The planks beneath me were seeping and the pole was dipping out of sight to find bottom. "I'll drown," I said. The river seemed to slant and tilt on edge. Sailor was poling the water fruitlessly and we were drifting sideways. The wind was rising and we were beginning to pitch and slop waves. Then the current caught us and we were swept up in a rush downstream. "Yeeoow!" Sailor was whooping. The raft was lifting and slapping back down and the wind was whipping the spray. "Yeeoow! Let 'er buck!" he was yelling and I was being pulled to the side. A force was drawing me and I couldn't stop. I had no balance and the force was going to pull me over and suck me under and Sailor was telling me, "You oughta learn to swim. I could throw you in and sink or swim, you'd learn pretty fast that way." He was eyeing me. Then he made a move toward me and I started clawing the air. But he didn't touch me. He moved back and the next thing I knew the current was leaving us in the shallows and we were drifting. "Now ain't you ashamed," Sailor said.

·   ·   ·

The place by the river was marked by big boulders and tall sycamores, and a narrow trail led down to it. A white cliff faced the other side and there was grass to sit on. Along the marshy bank, reeds and cattails. The water was clear and smooth and the river at this point was in a bend, not wide. It might have been an old swimming hole. A piece of rope was still knotted around a reaching limb overhead.

This spot was later developed into a camping ground with electrical hookups and toilets, but back then it was open and anybody's and you could think of it as personal and private. The names I carved on one tree can still be seen today. BOBBY/HOMINY. But you have to look. A hundred names since have also been carved.

I got there early and sat looking at the river. The dark holes under the roots in the water would make good places for catfish. In the marshy parts green snakes would be looking for the frogs. Above the cliff on the other side a couple of hawks glided. A few spirals of gnats hung in the air. I thought the bed of the river was probably limestone; the water looked so clean.

I forgot about time.

Then Hominy was spreading her apron on the grass and sitting down beside me.

"I like it here," she said. "I come here and just sit."

"It's peaceful," I said.

We were quiet for a while.

She was sitting with her knees up and her arms resting across them. Her skirt was loosely showing her legs and she didn't seem to care or be aware. She appeared both natural and reckless and not at all conscious of me. But my senses were alive to her, to the faint scent of violets on her skin, the shine in her hair, her soft breathing, the bright wet red of her lips. I felt lured. Her legs were golden.

She slipped off her shoes and dipped her feet in the water and I did the same, scattering the minnows, and then we felt them come back and nibble at our toes.

We touched with our feet, but when I tried to hold her hand, she pulled away, and I didn't try again.

"Okay," she said, "it's time to learn—" She'd brought a writing tablet and pencil with her purse and had it ready in her lap. "What was it? Double something?"

"Double negatives."

"Yeh, I gotta know about them." Her pencil was poised.

I went through the nots and don'ts and nothings,

giving her the right and wrong ways, and she wrote and repeated out loud. "'I don't have nothing' is wrong. 'I don't have anything' is right." She was concentrating and writing it down. "'That's not nothing' is wrong. 'That's not anything' is right."

It didn't take her long. "I see it. I get it," she said, and she suddenly became very still. She didn't exactly look at me, but past me, and she was seeing something in her mind.

"It's different too," she said. "It makes you feel different." A faraway tone in her voice.

"How do you mean?"

"Nothing is nothing. Anything is more like everything. You say not nothing and that's what it feels like. You say not anything and that's more. It's like the anything takes away the not. I don't know, it's more. It feels better."

"Yeh, a negative is like a subtraction probably."

"And a double negative is a double subtraction."

"Yeh, probably." I was agreeing, but she was seeing something I wasn't.

"And when it's not negative, what is it?"

"I dunno—positive?"

Her face widened and shone. "Yeah, positive."

"Well, a negative is a negative, and you put two of 'em together and that makes it double, you know, a double negative—" I think I was trying to understand more myself, but I ran out of reasoning..

"You don't have to keep talking." She was still looking past me, her face strangely happy. In another moment she said, "I'm never going to say not nothing again."

"Well, it's probably okay. A lot of people do. I only studied the rules, so—"

"No!" Her eyes clicked. "Not nothing feels like nothing. I hate that."

I didn't try to reply. The double negative had struck some chord with her, and it had a meaning for her that was beyond me.

"I got too far to go," she said. "I gotta start lightening the load."

"What load?" She was so pretty.

"The garbage I been dragging around, all the shit. I gotta get rid of it—Jesus!" She squeezed her eyes and clenched her teeth. "I get so sick and fed up sometimes!"

She started wagging her head and rocking herself. I thought she might cry, that she was holding back, and I was afraid to touch her. From a strangely happy state, her mood had shifted to this, to some kind of personal misery, and it happened so quick I felt caught.

I was used to Sailor's moods. He could switch just like that too, but this was different.

I inched closer and touched her arm. "Hey."

Her hand reached blindly and clutched at my arm. It was the same as she'd done on the side of the road. Her hand released and clutched again. It was like a baby's hand reaching from a crib. It was something helpless, instinctive.

Then she steadied, and pulled away.

"You okay?" I said.

"Don't touch me." Her head was turned.

I eased back. "I just asked."

"I'm all right." But she was still turned away. Then she tossed her head and took a breath. "I'm sorry. I gotta quit that shit too."

"If there's anything I can do—"

"What could you do?" A question, not sarcastic.

"I don't know. If I could help, I'd like to."

"I don't know what it'd be." She picked at the grass.

"Maybe you just need to talk."

She shook her head.

"If you wanted to tell me what's bothering you—"

"No." Her eyes were moving, flitting. She pulled the grass nervously. "I can't tell."

"Some things—"

"Just stop it, will ya? I don't want to talk to you. Not right now. And maybe not ever. So quit trying to get me to. When I got something to say, I'll let you know, okay?"

"Okay." But I didn't like her tone. It was too hard.

The rays of the sun were getting long and the lengthening light changed the spirals of gnats into wispy ghosts. The hawks above the cliff circled away. A turtle's head broke the surface of the water in the river and submerged again.

Hominy lay back on the grass, and I did too. And for a long time that was it.

"I'm sorry," she said. "You were just trying to be nice."

"I don't guess I know how to take you— Or maybe you take me wrong sometimes." My hands were behind my head and I was looking up at the sky.

"I got my moods," she said.

"Well, you can have 'em, I don't care, you don't have to jump on me."

She laughed, a small laugh, a kind of chuckle.

"What?" I didn't look.

"I like that. You take up for yourself, don'tcha?"

"I don't like getting jumped at."

"But you don't get mad."

"Sometimes I do."

"You're not rough, though."

"I might be."

"You haven't been with me."

"Well—you're different."

A moment. Something was between us. I could feel it, and my heart was pumping.

She turned to me on her side and put her hand on my stomach. "Want me to make you feel good?" Softly. Her hand was moving down.

"I don't know." I felt strangely in turmoil.

"You didn't like it?"

"Maybe not that way again."

"Whataya want?"

"I don't know." But I did. I wanted to put my arms around her and hold her and kiss her. I wanted to feel her body soaking into mine.

But it didn't happen like that.

She rolled back and arching, raised her hips, pulled her dress up and slipped off her panties.

"C'mon," she said. She was naked from the waist down, her legs slightly spread.

I put my hand on her thigh and my hand started trembling. Her skin was cool and felt like satin. My palm burned at the touch.

"You don't have to play around, just do it," she said.

I fumbled at my pants. Both my hands were shaking. Then I eased between her legs and she didn't move, only to turn her head to the side. When I tried to kiss her, she put her forearm between our faces.

"I love you," I said.

Her eyes were open and vacant, looking off.

It didn't take long.

The sun was going down.

Hominy stripped and slipped naked into the river. It seemed she almost hurried to get in, to get clean.

I sat and watched and felt a kind of wonderment. There was a flow, a smoothness inside me. Her body dipped and rose from the water, glistening. She was liquid and her skin was silken and gleaming in the falling light. I knew now what she was like and I wanted the feel and smell of her to remain. Her hair shone black and slick in the river. I'd found my way and gone right in. She was coming up bobbing, lifting, her breasts streaming rivulets. I had sunk down in her and slipped into the dark. Her arms were splashing oars out there, splashing white. I'd seen a bright streak, a beautiful sliver of light, and there was an explosion, a sound, and then a glow all around, pulsing, spurting outward. She was diving. There was calmness beneath that surface, a stillness floating down. I wanted to stay right there and lie in peace, but she shoved at my chest. "You're done," she said. "Lemme up."

That's when she hurried to the river to wash me off.

Now she was standing on the bank letting the air dry her skin, little goose bumps all over. Her painted toenails were bright red dots in the green grass. She stood naturally naked and squeezed at the water in her hair. Her pink nipples were sticking up, looking hard. I loved the sight of her and the thought of her, that she was so shining.

"Sometime," I said, "I'd like to kiss you."

"What for?"

"I just want to."

She was smoothing the wetness down her legs with her palms.

1 1 4

"You don't want to, though, do you?" I said.

"What?"

"Kiss."

"I've been kissed."

"What about sex?"

"What about it?"

"You like it?"

"Do you?"

"Yeah. I think I do. I think I like it a lot."

"Good for you." She flapped her panties straight and stepped into them. Plain pink.

"I don't guess you were a virgin," I said.

She stopped with her dress. "What's with you?"

"I don't care. I just wanted to get it straight."

She went ahead with her dress. "I've never been a virgin."

"Never?"

"Not since I was nine."

"Nine?" I think I blinked. "You mean, nine years old?"

"Or eight. I forget." She was buttoning her dress.

I felt odd and she seemed to change in front of me. I don't know how. She appeared for a moment less new, and she was still pretty but I saw a poorer slope in her shoulders. Her jaw line was lower slung.

"What happened?" I said.

"I got used to it."

I didn't know how to go on with it, what to say. My feet looked pale and useless.

She moved behind me to get her purse. The impression where we had lain was still in the grass and she walked across it thoughtlessly. The places she stepped made tiny efforts to heave back up.

"Uh-oh," she said behind me. "How'd you bang your head?" She poked my lump and I ducked.

"I got hit with a rock," I said. "When I was leaving your back porch."

She had come to the side with her purse and was pulling out her comb. Her hand stopped.

"I couldn't see who did it," I said.

She sat down slowly and started combing her hair. "You don't know who it was then?"

"It was somebody you heard probably. They must've been still waiting, hiding in the bushes."

She pulled out a hand mirror and looked at her face. The air was twilight now and her image was rosy. Her eyes were dark.

I asked, "You know who it was?"

"Yeah." She rested her hands with the mirror in her lap. Then she bared her teeth. "Shit!"

"That soldier?"

"No, hell, no, not him—dammit!" She was angry.

"Well, somebody's hanging around."

"I know it."

"What do they want? What're they after?"

"They want to run everybody off, keep everybody away from me. They're trying to stop me."

"How do you mean, stop you?"

"They're trying to keep me alone and then maybe I'll give up. I know what they're doing." Her voice died.

"Who?"

She patted the small hand mirror on her leg absently. I could see her face visibly sagging. "My brother," she said. "I told you, he keeps coming around, and I can't keep him off."

"Why?"

"That's the way he is." She lowered her head.

"Maybe I could stand up to him for you."

"It wouldn't do no good."

"I could fight him."

"He wouldn't fight fair."

"I wouldn't either. I don't care."

"Yeh, but he'd probably kill you."

That stopped me.

"You can't help," she said. She had become small.

"I don't get it, I mean, he's your brother—"

"He's just my half brother. That's why we're different. But he thinks he's got the say-so and he won't give it up." She shook her head. "That's why I gotta get on away. He won't never give it up."

The light was fading fast now. Her face was half in shadows. "He must be pretty mean," I said.

"As long as he can find me, he won't never let go." Now she started speaking almost in a whisper, more to herself than me. "I know what I gotta do. And what I gotta be. I see it in my mind the way it oughta be, and I dream about it. Everything around me is clean and new, and I'm clean all over. The way it's been I forget about. I don't even remember. And nobody knows me. But they think I'm nice and they like me. Everywhere I go I'm smiling—" She was lost in her mind.

A light breeze had started. A tune was fluting in the cattails. A frog croaked and another answered.

Hominy straightened. "You think I'm talking funny, don't you?"

"No, I think it sounds good. You make it sound good."

"Thinking about it keeps me going."

"I don't know, though, about smiling everywhere you go."

"Well, that's just in my head. I know it's not like that."

"I don't think anybody smiles all the time."

"I was just trying to say the way it'll feel."

"I tried to smile for an hour one time. My face started hurting. A bug hit and stuck in my front teeth."

She laughed.

"I looked like the grill of a fifty model Ford." I saw myself that way and laughed too.

She shoved me playfully, laughing, and I goosed her back, and for a while we had some fun. We were both ticklish in the ribs, and she was stronger than she looked, but we didn't exactly wrestle.

Then I saw a movement across the river.

"Look," I whispered, and we stopped playing. A bobcat was coming down to the water to drink, stepping carefully, searching with its wide eyes. The tips of its pointed ears and whiskers were white. Its front paws appeared padded.

We sat quietly and watched.

The bobcat lowered its head and lapped. When it raised its face and looked around, we saw how the water dripped from its slack jaws. The tongue licked quickly.

Then it was gone and a stillness was left. The water that had been lapped was flat without a ripple.

Hominy stood up and smoothed her dress. "I gotta go."

"I'll walk you."

"No, I don't want you to."

"We could have a hamburger." I got up.

"I'm just going to go—I got things to do."

"You don't want your brother to see me."

"I don't want you to have to fight."

"Hominy—"

"Look, I'm going, you stay here. Maybe I'll see you tomorrow."

She started up the trail and I watched her go, almost a silhouette. As she disappeared, a red line across the horizon cut her in half but she didn't look back.

"Yeh, see ya," I said.

I was left with my thoughts. She filled my mind, it seemed, but a part of her I couldn't see at all. A dark part was not nothing and felt like that. Another slice was everything. The touch of her had burned my hand. I'd been trembling. Just do it, she said, and looked off. Then it had been easy, but without holding. I'd slipped down into the dark and felt good. I was smoothed inside. Then she was standing naked in the twilight. The river behind her was shimmering and her body was glistening. She was such a shining thing. I'd see that picture in my mind forever.

I carved our names on the tree.

.   .   .

The back door of the Belvedere was off the alley, and that's the way I went in so I wouldn't have to pass Lew.

As soon as I walked into my room, though, I was stopped. The bed had a different, fancier spread, and there was a new throw rug on the floor. A big picture of ocean surf jumped at me from the wall. Neat white towels lay folded on the chair and a vase of artificial flowers topped the dresser. The room was also cleaner and smelled fresher. The green wick of a deodorizer stuck up in a bottle on the bedside table. A little Snickers bar lay on my pillow. Then I saw a bathrobe in the closet and a pair of thong sandals.

"Don't be mad."

I jumped. Lew was behind me in the doorway, smiling nervously, his magnified eyes beaming.

"Dammit, Lew, I told you I didn't want you sneaking up on me!"

"I'm sorry. I thought you could hear me."

"And what is this anyway, all this stuff? What're those flowers doing here? I didn't rent a room with stinking flowers in it."

"They brighten your room, though."

"I don't like it brighter. And what's that damn thing in the closet?"

"That's when you take a bath, you can wear it down the hall."

"I can wear my own clothes down the hall. And I don't like candy bars sticking all over my bed."

"I just thought—"

"I don't care what you thought, I don't want you scratching and pecking around me."

His face had fallen, and he was holding his hands in front of him, like an invalid. "You don't have to get mad," he said.

"Well, what'd you think? I rented this room like it was, that's what I expected, and you've been in here behind my back messing it up."

"What about the picture?"

"I don't like oceans."

"But you don't have a window to look out—"

"I've been looking out all my life. I'm tired of looking out. Besides, what would I look out on here anyway—the damn alley?"

"I was only trying to fix it up a little."

"It was better the way it was."

"Yes, well, perhaps next time, before I do anything, I should ask."

"That's right, you damn perhaps should, and you don't need to ask because you don't need to do anything."

It dawned on me I was in charge. I was giving orders, and he was the first person I'd ever had I could do that with. He was accepting it too, just standing there.

"Get it straight," I said, "when I want anything from you, I'll let you know, okay?"

"I understand." He crossed the room meekly and picked up the flowers. "I'll take these away." He was looking at me, hurt, and with the vase held at his waist, the flowers came up to his neck. He looked like he was peeking out of a petunia patch, some kind of wide-eyed little animal that wouldn't harm a soul.

He'd only tried to spruce the place up.

"Aw, hell, you can leave those," I said. "They're artificial, I don't guess I'll have to water 'em."

He set the vase back on the dresser.

"But the robe goes," I said. "You can take that for sure."

He folded the bathrobe over his arm. Then he hesitated.

"Now what?"

"Maybe I shouldn't mention it—" He was blinking, ready to flinch.

"Go ahead, mention what?"

"Well, if you're hungry—" He ducked his head. "I fixed your supper too."

Lew lived in a couple of rooms behind his office. One was probably a bedroom, but the door to that was closed. The room he opened to me was a kitchen and everything else. My first impression was that I'd stepped into somebody's personal flea market, the place was so cluttered, but also sort of arranged.

"You *live* here?" I said.

"Come in, come in, sit down. Everything's ready to

serve. It won't take a minute." He was fidgety and happy.

But I didn't know where to sit. The place was crammed everywhere with curiosities. Shelves and tables were loaded with little statues of dogs and cats, owls and elephants, birds, you name it. There was a ceramic collection of billygoats with beards, a corner stacked with lacquered music boxes. Baskets, jars and vases, plastic fruit and flowers. The walls were covered solid with pictures and plaques and framed quotations. There were a thousand dinky things like in a variety store and a work table at the window was junked with cans of paste, brushes and paint and hand tools, the stuff you use for hobbies. A straw nest in the middle of the table was filled with egg-shaped rocks painted different colors.

"Sit there," he said, indicating a small place set for two with plates and napkins.

I sat carefully in the chair while Lew fussed in the kitchen behind a divider. "Whataya do," I asked, "collect all these things?"

He didn't hear. He was rattling pans and dishes.

Then the food appeared, chicken on a platter, carrots on the side, peas in a bowl. White, orange, and green.

"A gourmet delight," he said.

And the peas looked normal, but the carrots were long fingers dripping a kind of clear glue. They appeared slick and sticky. The chicken was different too, and it might have been half cooked. The skin was slippery on the meat and all of it was poured with a thick yellowish gravy. Different humps of chicken in the gravy still looked alive.

"That's a very mild curry sauce," he said. "I hope you like it."

I didn't want to touch it.

"The carrots are my own recipe, sweet and sour."

Slick and nasty.

"You're not eating," he said.

"I don't think I'm hungry."

"Something wrong?"

"I don't think I want anything right now."

"But try some, have a taste." He was sitting across from me with his fork and knife poised, his two little fingers sticking out, his elbows tucked in close at his sides. "Please do."

I picked at the chicken and took a bite. The pale meat was like mush, an unnatural pulp in my mouth, and I had to swallow hard to get it down.

"You don't like it," he said.

I pushed my plate back. "Lew, I don't think I can eat that stuff."

His face was disappointed. "I'm sorry, you don't like chicken."

I was used to my meat roasted over a fire until it was crispy and crackling, the fatty parts charcoaled. What was in front of me was runny looking.

"I don't want to hurt your feelings," I said.

"I'll fix you something else. What would you like?" He was trying to please.

"I don't want anything. You go ahead."

"I can't eat without you."

"I told you I'm not hungry."

We went back and forth, and finally I convinced him. "I mean it, go on and eat, don't worry about me."

"Well, if you're sure—" He sliced delicately with the tip of his knife and lifted the bite with his fork in his left hand.

I wasn't going to stay much longer, but I didn't

want to act impolite either. He'd gone to some trouble. I swept my hand around. "Where do you get all this?"

"Oh, I collect. I go around and find things. I see things I like, I pick them up. Sort of a hobby." He was trying to smile. "And I have my little projects over there." He indicated the work table. "I get my ideas from some of my materials. Right now I'm finishing a bird's nest with eggs. I found some rocks shaped like eggs, but I'm putting my own design on them. Then I have a bunch of feathers I found. I'll fashion those into a bird and put it on the nest."

"And then what do you do?"

"Oh, I keep busy. I'm never idle for things to do."

"I mean, what do you do with the stuff you make?"

"I sell some. At the festival, for instance, I'll set up a table and have some of my items for sale there. You'd be surprised what people will buy." He was eating his carrots. "These are delicious. Sure you won't try some?"

I shook my head. "So that's what you do," I said, "and then you run this place."

"Well, actually, this hotel was a piece of property my family owned, but I've taken it over."

"This is your hometown then."

"Oh, yes, I've lived here all my life." Proudly.

"With your family."

"There's just my older sister and me now. But we don't see each other. You know, she's a recluse. And it's a pity, she was such a pretty girl when she was younger. She turned out strange. But then strangeness ran in our family, I think." He looked straight at me now. "You know, some people consider me a little strange."

"Well, maybe you are." That slipped out.

But he only smiled. "Yes, by normal standards I

suppose I am." He went back to his food. "But if that's the way I am, then that's the way I am. Who's to judge?"

"Well, you probably have your own friends that like you—"

"No, I can't say that I do. I've lived here all my life, this is my home, but I can't say that I have any friends." He said that plainly and didn't seem at all bothered.

I still wanted to smooth it. "You keep yourself busy, though, making things, collecting—"

"Oh, I'm never lonely." He said that too quickly, too brightly. Which meant he really was.

But loneliness comes from a long way back. It's as old as creation, perhaps a condition of creation itself, Sailor said, and you let it have its uses. You don't let it make you feel sorry.

I felt the clutter closing in on me now, and I didn't want to keep sitting. I pushed back from the table. "Well, I gotta go. I enjoyed the visit."

"You don't have to run." He was suddenly anxious.

"Yeh, I do. I got a couple of things I need to see about." I stood up.

"Let me fix you something else, a steak?"

"No, I'm really not hungry."

"I'm sorry you didn't like the chicken."

"Well, it was probably all right—"

"Take some with you."

"No, thanks. I'll see ya." I started for the door.

"I was going to show you some of my collections."

"Maybe some other time." I was going.

He pursued right behind me. "I'm sorry you have to leave—do you have your key?"

"Yeah, I got my key." But that irritated me—did I have my key? A hen's peck.

"You have clean towels."

"I know."

"I'll leave your light on."

That broke it and I turned. "Leave my light alone, okay?"

"I just thought—"

"I don't care, leave things alone. I don't want you bothering me. And I don't want you fixing me any more gourmet delights either. You got that?"

"I'm sorry." Head down.

"Then just quit it." I stomped out through his office and left him with his clutter, his little worthless objects, his gluey carrots and slippery chicken, feathers and egg rocks and silly mothering ways. Jesus! No wonder he didn't have friends.

.   .   .

I paid a visit to Judy and Mawd in the pasture near the fair grounds. They were still grazing, but they had ranged in a circle the length of their ropes, so I staked them in a different spot, still near the stream where they could drink.

Then I stayed awhile for company, and it was all so familiar, the sound of their mouths pulling the grass hard and munching, Judy to the right of Mawd, their heads down, feeding slowly one step at a time, big bodies on slender legs, shifting their weight smoothly. A new moon showed their forms darker than the trees and the little stream was slightly rushing, a breaking streak of silver in the black field.

It was a peaceful time. They were such simple creatures in their minds and habits, in simply being.

Their living was just that. But with feelings still. At times almost human. I sensed the pull of their easy mood, their strength at rest. There was an attachment, a kind of invisible flow between us, but I couldn't name it. A shared life, the hidden magnet in blood, I didn't know, something was there. And I wondered if they dreamed.

If they did, it was probably of pulling logs and being hitched to a wagon, straining with a load uphill. They'd been made to work all their lives.

Or maybe, because of that, they'd dream of flying and clouds like meadows, of cool breezes and starry nights.

Yeah, that was better—but I didn't want to get too sentimental, so I left it at that.

"We're gonna win that contest," I told them. "We can do it." I rubbed their noses and patted their shoulders and told them good night.

I stopped next at the fair grounds. It was deserted and shadowy in the night, but the area for the pulling event was marked off and I wanted to see that.

The place was beyond the show barn and it was a big oval with five rows of bleachers on two sides where people could sit. There was an entrance for the teams at one end and an exit at the other.

The sled to be pulled was there too, a long iron bed with smooth runners. The weight in cement blocks would be placed on it and a team would have three chances to pull the load ten feet. You'd draw first for position and each team would go in turn. After a full round, more weight would be added, and the teams in turn would keep pulling a heavier sled until they couldn't and were eliminated. The distance you had to pull would be measured automatically with a string, a ten-foot length with one end tied to the rear of the sled and the other end to a stick stuck in the ground right next to the back end. When the sled was pulled, the string would pay out its length and jerk the stick from the ground. You'd unhitch your team then and wait your turn for the next round with a heavier load, and that's the way it would go until somebody won. A tractor would drag the sled back after each pull to the starting point to keep the contest going in the same short course.

While Sailor backed Judy and Mawd to the sled, it would be my job to hitch the singletrees, then get out front and line the team straight to the load. So I'd be the helper and Sailor the driver.

I imagined the oval strung with waving pennants, the bleachers crowded with people cheering and urging the teams on. With the loads getting heavier and the teams starting to drop out, the contest would get exciting. The ground would start getting chewed up with stomping hooves. Then the contest would narrow down to three or four teams, then two, and finally the winner, the champion.

The record pull was 3800 pounds. A span of big brown mules from Springfield had done that. But Judy and Mawd had pulled heavier timber over rougher ground in the hills.

There was no doubt in my mind. When you flicked the reins and asked for their best, Judy and Mawd would give all they had. They'd pull their hearts out.

Next, I went to the café and ate a double cheeseburger, two orders of French fries, and a thick slice of cherry pie à la mode. I thought I could feel come features coming back in my face, it all tasted so good.

But now I had nothing to do. The closed stores fronted the street like a row of silent faces staring from behind dark glasses.

In the trees, it seemed, there was always something—the fires and cooking, the mules, the familiar chores of washing and mending, and the life searching and flying that never stopped. Even with the days the same, the woods were busy, never at loose ends.

But here, in the middle of town, where things were supposed to be interesting and happening, nothing was. A few cars roamed idly, and that was about all. There was nothing to occupy my hands and I felt personally robbed.

I stood awhile and pretended to observe.

Then I decided I had business to attend to, and I started walking purposefully. A serious matter was involved. I remembered I was supposed to meet some guy at the pool hall. Damn, how could I forget? I'd have to hurry now or I'd miss him.

I moved faster with a definite objective in mind.

But I got there too late. Only two tables were being played out of ten, and except for a couple of loafers and the manager watching from the side, the poolroom was empty. I stretched my neck to see in the far corner, but my man wasn't there. I must have just missed him.

I went to the pay phone on the wall and dialed a number. It rang but there was no answer. I changed the number around in my head and dialed again.

This time a man's voice answered. "Hullo."

"Bill?"

"Who?"

"Is this Bill?"

"Bill who?"

"Bill Thompson."

"Nobody here by that name. What number you calling?"

I told him the number.

"Well, that's this phone," he said, "but no Bill's here."

"Are you sure?"

"I just told ya. What would I lie for? Nobody named Bill lives here."

"If you see him, tell him I called."

"What're you talking about? How'm I gonna see him? I don't know nobody named Bill Thompson."

"Tell him I'll meet him at the usual place."

"What place? Look, are you pulling my leg? Who is this?"

"Just tell him if he can't come up with the money this time, the deal's off."

"What the hell're you talking about? Who is this?"

"I can't wait any longer, so you tell him, he's got one hour and that's it. I'm not fooling around any longer." I hung up.

As I walked out, the two loafers were looking at me curiously, but I didn't pretend to notice. They'd just have to wonder.

Then out to the roller rink.

But this time it was closed, and the canvas sides were rolled down loosely, billowing in the breeze. The surrounding graveled parking area was bleak and gray in the moonlight. Still, I could hear the traffic of the skates in the air, their rough whirling and clicking sounds. The memory of those sounds had remained in place, I supposed, and always would. They were so fixed in that location they'd have nowhere else to go. I threw a few handfuls of gravel at the canvas sides and headed back to town.

.　　.　　.

The green car moved down the street a block away, turned a corner, and glided out of sight in the dark. I was at the service station, drinking a Coke, and I couldn't see exactly, but two heads appeared to be behind the wheel. Which meant the driver had someone pressed warmly to his side. And if the driver was the soldier, that someone might have been Hominy. He'd given her a ride to work that morning and she wouldn't let me walk her from the river. She had things to do, she said.

I felt my stomach harden.

A moment later a pickup turned the same corner and disappeared in the same direction. It was the junky thing with the sideboards and chicken wire that I'd seen earlier, that belonged to the river rats. It was following the green car, it seemed, but at a distance not to be noticed. Even a block away I heard the sputter of the motor misfiring.

There was a sputter of thoughts in my mind too, but I couldn't figure it.

Then I became aware of an occasional sharp sound on the side and behind the service station where there was an empty lot. A rock was hitting a telephone pole back there. And a few seconds later another one hit. Not hard. But pointedly and definitely. Someone was throwing from behind the building. I couldn't see but the rocks were hitting the mark every time, they were thrown with such accuracy. I could see them only after they hit and flipped in the air, but that was enough to tell where they came from.

Then they stopped. No more rocks. There was a sudden stillness around the pole and I waited. The person throwing those rocks was also the one who'd thrown the rock at my head, I felt that for certain, and if he came at me now, I was going to be ready.

But no one appeared and I heard no movement. The man in the station cleaning the grease rack was the only action, and the air compressor chugging the only noise.

A car pulled in for gas. An old man.

I finally made a swing to the side of the station to look and make sure. Slowly, carefully—some oil drums, nothing behind them, a few old tires, trash, a ruined engine block. But no rock thrower. Hominy's half brother, that's who it had to be, had vanished in the night.

It was spooky. He'd been trying to scare me, using the cover of dark, staying out of sight, but with the rocks letting me know. He was bothering Hominy so she couldn't have her own life, scaring people off, so she'd have to be alone.

But rocks—what kind of thing was that? What kind of dull instinct? That's what people used when they were dropping from trees and still half ape, not even civilized. That's when people used rocks.

But the rock thrower out of sight also could have been anybody, and nothing had happened, so I let it go and paid a call at Dominoes.

Sailor was at the back table again with his whiskey and cards and he was having his fun, but not the same as before. This time his eyes were already glazed over and his jaws were sagged and he wasn't winning. There were only a few wadded bills in front of him. Still, he was trying to put up a front and he didn't care if he lost.

I felt sad, watching him, and I realized for the first time that the thing for him was the playing. Not the game. But he couldn't just play, not like that. He had to have the whiskey first to loosen him and then he could sit with other men and pretend to fit in and be somebody else, or finally himself, or something. I couldn't spot the person. But it was the playing, the communion in playing, and not the game. The winning or losing was only some kind of indifferent score to him.

I think I glimpsed him all at once as a waste. He had kept himself to himself and apart from others, except for this kind of bleary-eyed communion that claimed no ties and had no meaning. The cards were only numbered to ten with a few faces. The colors were simply two, the suits four. It didn't take a genius to figure the combinations or the odds. You could play one hand and forget it. But each hand was a new connection, a touch with someone else's. And that was the thing, a passing touch. Nothing more. You shuffled the deck and went on.

I didn't care to stay and watch, and I could tell Sailor wouldn't last much longer either. He was getting that far gone.

But he was still there when I left, smiling at the other players in general, betting and raising regardless, looking and not seeing.

If he was different ever, it was before I knew him and he knew me. But that would've been a different person and I couldn't imagine him that.

Now I was drawn. It might have started with the sadness I felt about Sailor, with the loneliness in the night, the darkness all around. The moon was there. And bits and pieces were flashing in my brain. The incidents had piled up and a thought stuck in my head, a type of question, I suppose, and I probably knew the answer, but I needed to see for myself, to prove the suspicion or doubt, if it was that. I couldn't put it into words, but I was definitely drawn to Hominy's.

When I got to her house, I circled quietly and made sure nothing was hiding in the bushes and that the green car was not parked anywhere near.

Then I slipped into the hedge beneath her window. There was no light on in her room. I tried to peek in but the sill was a fraction too high, so I listened instead with my ear against the wall and I heard a hum, a dull tone in the wall, or inside my head perhaps, but that's all. Nobody was home.

I slid my back down the wall and settled myself within the cover of the hedge. After a while, I think I dozed.

A car door slammed. The car roared away, screeching its tires. Then footsteps approached in the gravel drive. They were stepping lightly and passed the hedge within arm's reach. I was hidden, but I saw Hominy's bare calves, her bare feet in sandals. She was alone and I held my breath until she turned the corner at the back porch.

I heard the screen door squeak and close, then the click of the door to the house itself, her door next, and she was in her room. Her light went on and illuminated a patch of white in the drive and my hands and knees in the hedge leaves. Then she pulled down her shade, and she light around me yellowed.

I couldn't hear, but with my back against the wall I could feel her movement in the room, a crossing to the closet and back, to the bed, and I imagined her undressing.

Her light went off soon and the drive blinked to black. She was in bed. In a gown, or naked, I wondered. I imagined her lying on her back, eyes closed, lips parted, quietly falling to sleep, the outlines of her body soft in the dark.

I waited and held still.

Sure enough, a few minutes later stealthy sounds behind the house, someone hurrying across the backyard, and I was instantly alert and taut. The screen door squeaked, a board ached on the porch, padding sounds, not shoes, and the door to the house ticked. No sound for a moment, then her door yawned and someone had entered her room.

I felt myself straining. I wanted to hear some sound of contest, but none came through. The acceptance of the intruder was silence.

Then I felt it against my back, a faraway rhythm, a steady, almost regular pulse, a faint heaving motion in the distance. But it was my sense of that more than the actual feel. It was the bed grunting against the wall.

I felt something inside me turn off.

It seemed a long time before the rhythm suddenly stopped.

I moved from the hedge and into the bushes at the corner of the yard. My feet had dissolved and my chest was burning.

Soon a form glided from the house across the porch and through the screen. It paused, then darted like a shadow into the alley. The moonlight showed the dark figure bent and distorted.

It was, of course, Spoon Crane, and I knew.

All at once, like plates of food passed at a family table, the names passed before me. Spoon Bread, Ham Hock, Collard Greens, Hominy.

That was a complicated moment in my heart and I hung my head.

5

Lew had left the light on in my room, and I switched it off. He'd also left a sandwich on the dresser, a chicken thing cut catty-corner in half, and I didn't want it.

For a long time I lay wide-eyed awake on the bed and it seemed the dark room was full of roving minds. I was trying to figure it. She was so pretty. Her half brother, she said. The half had to account for the difference—her bright eyes and teeth, her wanting to get away and step up. She'd smelled clean and fresh and I could still feel her skin like satin. But she was moody and tough too. I'm gonna make it, she said, all the way. Till you live like you want to, I said. And I wanted to go with her. We could make it together. Hominy and me.

But I had jumped the gun. She had never said together. That was me and my wants going on ahead. Skipping the in-between. Just do it, she said. But don't touch, don't kiss. That was hard and closed off, like a part of her wouldn't work. The touching, feeling part. Like that part had been smashed in a wreck, but the way she looked covered the damage.

I was tossing on the bed, a sick feeling inside.

She'd been wronged. Since she was nine, she said. Or eight. She forgot. I got used to it, she said. A dark part of her was not nothing and felt like that. But the rest was shining. I was looking at her through cut-out holes with no face, and I could see her but she couldn't see me. She appeared half shadow and half light. When I shut one hole, she was all light. When I shut the other, she was all shadow. I could wink at her dark and bright. Good and bad. Clean and dirty. And the last I didn't like. The dirty. I had to shut that out. At nine you're bald and clean.

Hominy. Maybe if she changed her name. But it was her fault too. Her blame also. She still let him. Like an old habit. Even enduring, she still let him, and I felt ashamed for her.

You can fit some pieces together, to see, and try to understand, Sailor said, but you can't place blame. It's other things too. But what? Chance? Evil? It was beyond me. A river was high and running hard and I felt caught up and swept in the current. I couldn't swim and a force was pulling to suck me under.

Hominy. I was holding to her and I couldn't help it. I couldn't help my feelings. I was tossing in turmoil.

Then it was calm. We were in the shallows and drifting. I love you, I said. But she didn't go for that. I don't want to hear that crap, she said.

I slept finally in a nightmare.

. . .

The next morning in the bathroom mirror I saw, not a face exactly, but what looked like somebody's faint sketching of what could become one. I felt spriggles, and I could barely see brows and lashes beginning.

I still couldn't see me, but I felt a new hope. If I could imagine myself, it seemed, I might also look that way. It wouldn't hurt, and to make it right I could do it in parts. It didn't have to be complete all at once. I could start with the eyes I wanted, the nose, the mouth and chin, and then all together the set expression. I could imagine my features one at a time, keep them fixed in mind, and when they grew back, that's the way I'd look, the way I'd be.

So the lightning, after all, had been good. It had wiped the slate clean and I could become now what I imagined and when people looked at me, that's what they'd see, if they cared to look, the real me.

The thought made me feel good.

Then Lew wanted to feed me breakfast.

"I don't think so," I said. "I don't have time."

"But it's ready," he said. "I started when I heard you in the bathroom."

He had a place cleared at the end of his desk in his office, and I sat down. At least it wasn't back with all his knickknacks. That would've been depressing first

1 3 8

thing in the morning, to have a thousand statue objects all around, all dead.

He brought the breakfast on a tray. Bacon and eggs and English muffins. A jar of strawberry jam. A dish of butter. And, oddly, a fried banana. I'd never seen that before.

I picked up a piece of bacon. The edges were ripply, but the slice itself was straight and brittle.

"It's crisp," he said, smiling.

"But what happened?" The thing was also bone-dry. "Where's the grease?"

"I drained it on a napkin."

"What'd you do that for?"

"That's the way it's done. Don't you like it?"

"I like bacon greasy, the way it is."

"I'll fix you some more." He was anxious and hurt.

"Nah, forget it. I don't want bacon."

And I didn't want the eggs either. There were two, sunny-side up and laid on top of two muffin halves. The whites were almost clear liquid and the yellows looked milky. The fried banana was brownish and limp.

"Lew"—I pushed my plate away—"I hate to say it, but I don't think you know how to cook."

"Oh, but I do. It's my specialty."

"This doesn't even look like a breakfast."

"Perhaps not what you're used to—"

"Look at that banana—you ruined it."

"It's fried in peanut oil."

"The eggs could still hatch."

"If you'd like them more done—"

"Lew—I don't know what you're trying to do. You don't have to fix my meals, I told you."

"But I don't mind." He looked so frail and help-less. He just stood there holding his hands.

I felt pity for him. But that's all. I didn't want his cooking for me or anything else. "Well, let's just forget it." I stood up to leave. "I gotta go."

"I'm sorry," he said.

When I was down the hall, he called after me. "Will you be in early?"

I turned. "Dammit, Lew, will you cut that out! You're not my damn mother!"

"I'm sorry." He ducked his head. "I like you, that's all. I worry about you."

"Well, don't. Pick on somebody else. You're mak-ing me jumpy, and I don't like it."

"I'm sorry."

"And quit saying you're sorry."

"Okay." Eyes blinking, face twitching. "I'll try."

"Jesus!"

The guy was hopeless. He'd upset my good feelings about my new face too.

.   .   .

Friction or balance, you see, that's the thing. You get outta balance, you run into friction, and that just wears you down. So you gotta have balance, and if you quit thinking about it, it'll come to you. Then you can feel a little grace. That comes free with the balance. Sailor talk-ing. With the ax. With the swing? I said. With anything, he said.

.   .   .

The counter was like a narrow strip of hardwood floor, solid, varnished, and smooth as glass. I've sat at a thousand counters since, but Hominy's in the drugstore is the one that's fixed in my mind. It was *L*-shaped, with fifteen pedestal stools bolted to the floor, three fountainheads sticking up in the middle, and a mirror across the wall behind. Napkin holders with rounded tops. Tin ashtrays. Tall boxes of plastic drinking straws. Small posters of ice cream, banana splits, and sodas were Scotch-taped around the mirror. A two-pot coffee machine off-center. It was an ordinary drugstore, except for the old-fashioned fountains sticking up like the necks of geese.

Hominy brought me coffee without asking, and once again her eyes were a little red and smudged.

"Morning," I said.

"Morning." Her voice was indifferent.

"I'll have a doughnut too," I said.

"Glazed or chocolate?"

"Glazed—and chocolate."

"Both?"

"Yeh—please."

She moved smoothly, but there was a difference now, a posture in her hips, a new slant in her shoulders—an attitude maybe. Something about her was definitely altered in a passing glance. There was some strain of her background in her bearing, a hint of family resemblance. At the same time, it wasn't there. She was too pretty, too unlike what she came from, and there was no comparison.

She brought the doughnuts.

"That soldier," I said. "What's his name?"

"Whataya wanna know for?" She was stopped.

"I guess I just want to know if you like him or not."

"You keep asking that."

"Well, I want to know. Is he a regular boyfriend, or what?"

"It's none of your business."

"What if I make it my business?"

"Ha!" She put her hands on her hips. "You try it."

"Well, just tell me his name."

She glared at me, then shrugged. "His name's Darryl."

"Darryl." I had to sneer. "That's a dumb name."

"And yours ain't. Buudd." She made it sound like heavy mud.

"My real name's Bobby."

"Yeah, Booby." She walked away.

I chomped into my doughnuts. I hadn't meant to start an argument, but she'd acted so indifferent, as if we'd never met. That got me. I didn't want to argue with her, though. I wanted it easy between us and natural. I wanted us to feel good together, even now.

She was walking back by.

"Hey, I'm sorry," I said.

"So what?" She was digging into a box for something.

"I mean it."

"So? Big deal."

"I don't want you mad at me. Okay?"

She raised. "Then quit asking questions. I don't have to answer to you."

"I guess I just don't like you going with him, Darryl."

"You don't know I do."

"You were with him again last night." I shouldn't have said that, but it was out before I thought.

Her eyes bored into me. "How do you know that?"

"I know." I couldn't look at her.

"You been sneaking around on me."

"I thought I saw you in his car, in town."

"You're lying."

"No, I saw his car in town, and I thought you were in it." Now I looked at her and she was waiting. I went on, "Then I was at your house. I knew when you came home."

Her eyes were moving. But no expression.

"I saw your brother too."

Her lips parted. Her hand went slowly to her stomach. Then she turned mechanically and walked away.

I stared at my coffee. A false sense of distance loomed before me. My hands seemed far away. The back counter was a farther rim. The counter itself stretched into a plain. I had hurt something and it wasn't just feelings. It was deeper than that. I knew, I said. I saw. The truth. The hardest thing. And I had spoken the truth like an ordinary fool.

Hominy came back and her hand jerked, writing my check.

"I'm sorry," I said.

"I don't like people sneaking around on me." Her voice was strained and hoarse.

"I didn't mean to."

"I don't like you now." She cut her eyes at me and they were hateful.

"We can get away. We can go to Dallas together, if you still want to."

"There's a law against Peeping Toms. I could have you throwed in jail."

"I won't do it again."

"I don't want to see you again, never, you hear?" Her mouth was pinched. Her chin was quivering.

"I want to help."

"And if you tell anybody—" Her eyes suddenly glistened and I thought she was going to cry, but she squeezed them shut and shook her head.

I stretched my hand, but I couldn't reach her. "Hominy, hey," I whispered. I felt people looking.

She didn't cry, though. She gained control and straightened.

"We can leave here," I said. "We can get away from this place and get away from your brother."

"But now you know." She was looking down, weaker.

"I don't care, though. You're still good."

"No, I'm not." Ashamed.

"Yes, you are—"

She took a breath and became stronger. "Why don't you just leave? You keep sitting here, talking, taking up my time, you're going to get me fired. I gotta keep working."

"When you get off, I'll meet you by the river."

"No." Definitely.

"Please, we could talk."

"I don't wanna talk, not about nothing, and I don't wanna be around you no more. I don't like you looking at me."

"I'm not looking at you—"

"I know what you think."

"I'm trying to tell you—"

"Just go on, will ya? Leave me alone. I mean it, I don't like you now." Her eyes were flitting.

"I could help. I want to."

"Shit!" Her mouth twisted. "Some help you are." Then her eyes turned blank and for a moment she stared. Her voice flattened strangely and she said, "But it ain't you, is it?"

"When you get off," I said, "meet me."

She shook her head and her focus came back. "I don't want you around me. I gotta think now. I gotta have some time."

"When then?"

"I dunno. Not for a while maybe." She was moving away. "I gotta work." She was holding, continuing.

It was left like that.

But I still felt a chance, that we could go on and forget the truth. We could leave what was behind and let it disappear. It could be a blank spot in the past or somebody else's memory.

And I could understand if she needed time alone for a while. The hardest things do.

.   .   .

I called the sawmill from the pay phone at the service station.

Chubb sounded irritated. "You were just out here yesterday, hell."

"You told me to check back."

"I know it, but not every ten minutes."

"How 'bout tomorrow?"

"Goda'mighty, boy, give it some time, a couple of days, hell, ain't gonna be nothing right now, I told you, we're caught up."

"I want a job, though."

"I know you do. I got your application, hell, I'll keep you in mind."

"A couple of days then, you think there might be an opening?"

"Not before then. But, yeh, in a couple days maybe. We got some loads supposed to be coming in."

"Okay, I'll call you in a couple of days."

"Yeh, you do that. But, Jesus, not every ten minutes."

.   .   .

On the way to the café I had to cross an alley opening between buildings, and that's where Spoon Crane stopped me. As I was stepping from the sidewalk, he jumped out suddenly and blocked me.

"Goin' somewheres?"

His face appeared deformed. It was bruised purple and swollen widely across the nose where Sailor had slammed him, and his upper lip was split and ballooned.

I froze. In the corner of my eye, Collard and Ham back in the alley, an impression of chicken wire at their heads, their pickup behind them.

My body had tightened and turned cold.

"Them mules was ours," Spoon said. A filthy gap showed in his mouth where Sailor had also knocked out a snag of tooth.

I held tight and felt my neck warming.

"You was the one that run and told Sailor about 'em, wasn't ya? You got him to bluff Sanders off us, didn't ya?" His eyes were dead and he kept them on me, slowly twisting his neck. A snake's head. "So now you owe us," he said.

I'd seen that head at night, distorted in moonlight.

Then he was talking and I wasn't hearing. I was at the house again in the dark with my back against the wall and I was feeling the bed grunting through the wall.

"—and you better stay away from her," I heard him say. "That's mine—"

And that's when I struck, and his eyes popped and

his head went back with his mouth gaping. The feel of broken bone beneath his swollen nose shot into my fist and he was lurching back with his hands to his face, with blood spurting between his fingers. He shrieked in pain and Collard and Ham were on me. They were clawing at me and tried to grab hold, but I was swinging and throwing them off and they couldn't hold me. They were like dogs snapping and jumping back, but Spoon's screaming was in between and they were fearful too, and I was wild, too wild for them. And then a voice shouted, and a car was stopping, and I broke free and ran.

I didn't stop until I was at Pauline's and safe inside her iron fence. Then I was shaking and spent and I fell down in her drive.

Sailor was still passed out, Pauline was sleeping, and the rest of the house was quiet, but Stella, the old cleaning woman, let me wait in the big room.

A TV was in the corner and I watched game shows. They all seemed the same, with contestants jumping up and down and squealing, they'd get so excited, but there were some good prizes at stake, and I tried to answer questions along with the contestants.

I ended up winning a supply of dog food, some cookware, and two free dance lessons at Arthur Murray's, not a thing I could really use, except maybe the dance lessons, but I didn't know when that would be.

I decided it took a certain type of mind for game shows. You had to think fast on your feet and I wasn't good at that. You also had to be good at details and my brain saw pictures, scenes overall, so the game shows weren't for me.

But watching them passed the time and allowed me to settle down.

I'd instinctively run to Sailor, where I knew he'd be, and I didn't feel particularly big about that, but the Cranes were born river rats, mean and vicious, and what if they'd gotten me down? They were biters and gougers, and I could see it. They would've kicked me in the head and stomach, stomped my balls, clawed me, bitten my nose off, and gouged out one of my eyes. That's the way they did. They'd leave a body maimed and mutilated for life.

So I was lucky. But I had slammed Spoon's nose where it was already broken and he wouldn't forget. Even if he'd started it, he'd still want to pay me back for that. And he didn't want me with Hominy—

I decided to go back to camp with Sailor. To let it cool. I'd take a couple of days. Then come back for the pulling contest and start again. I'd feel better.

But I was still going on my own. That was settled.

Stella came through once, vacuuming the carpet, her crippled hands pushing the handle regularly back and forth, and she never seemed to look up. She was a kind of steady cleaning machine herself, and I wondered, when she was younger and pretty, did she ever have fun? When she was with the miners in Colorado, did she ever smile?

When she came to my chair, I lifted my feet, and she worked under them with her machine and went on. The TV was fuzzed while she vacuumed, but I kept watching.

Later, Pauline stopped in the room. "Well, looky here," she said, "ol' lonesome you—whatcha doin'?"

"Just waiting, for Sailor."

"Looks like. Same ol' story, huh?"

"I guess." I was just sitting. I'd turned the TV off with the soap operas.

She smiled. Her dress was white with slits up the sides and her face was made up with long eyelashes and spots of rouge on her cheeks. Her orange hair was frizzy and wild and I guessed she purposely combed it that way.

"It's after lunch," she said. "You hungry?"

"Not very." Her high heels made her taller than I remembered, but the slices of her thighs showing through the slits were the same, round and dimpled.

"C'mon," she said, "let's go to the kitchen."

I followed the saucy swing in her hips.

She had me sit at the table. "I'll fix you something. Whataya want?"

"I dunno." I didn't feel hungry. The soft tops of her breasts were pooched out of her dress and jiggling when she walked.

"How 'bout a sandwich? We got baloney."

"Okay."

"Mustard or mayonnaise?"

"Mayonnaise—please."

She poured me a glass of milk and started with the sandwich next to the sink. A black cat on top of the refrigerator again waved its tail and watched her. And I did too. She stood with her legs spread in a solid stance. Her dress was tight against her hips and her big body tapered down into surprisingly trim ankles. There was a small bruise on the back of her left arm. From a bump probably, but I imagined some man's hand.

She glanced at me. "You seen Sailor yet today?"

"No."

"I think he's sick. And I don't mean just drunk, you know what I mean?"

"Well, he can look pretty bad sometimes, but he gets over it."

"Maybe he has. But he's got something wrong with him."

"I don't know."

She was slicing a tomato, looking at that. "He got any insurance?"

"Whataya mean?"

"Hospital, burial insurance, anything like that? He probably doesn't."

"No, none of that."

"How 'bout a bank account, savings?"

"No."

"You got any relatives?"

I shook my head.

She shifted her weight. "Then you got a problem."

"How do you mean?" Her tone had changed slightly. I felt a different atmosphere between us.

She cut up a piece of baloney in a dish and set it for the cat on the refrigerator, and the cat looked at it without interest.

"I don't want him croaking here," Pauline said.

She sounded casual. "He probably just looks bad," I said. "He'll get better."

She set my sandwich in front of me. "I didn't ask you if you liked lettuce."

"Yeh, that's fine." There was a lot of lettuce and a thick slab of baloney with tomatoes.

"Look," she said, "I got nothing against Sailor. He's all right with me, but if he croaks I don't want his body found here. Understand?" She stood over me with one hand on the back of my chair. A warmth from her body came down.

"He won't, though. He gets well every time," I said.

"Maybe. But lemme tell you something, if he don't and he clicks off here, you got him, understand? You can drag him out in the street and say he dropped dead there, I don't care. I ain't having no corpse picked up here."

"I guess it would look bad."

"Honey, a dead body never earned me a dime, and I don't need the advertisement."

"He'll be all right, though. I've seen him in bad shape lots of times."

The front doorbell rang and Pauline looked at her watch. "That's gotta be Charlie. Wouldn't you know it, right on the dot, just like a Virgo." She was moving away.

At the kitchen door, she turned. "Sailor don't get up in another hour, you better take a look. He's yours." She gestured. "You want, fix yourself another sandwich." She walked out.

The front door was opened and I heard Pauline's voice down the hall. "Charlie, you ol' sonofabitch, I've been waiting—"

Charlie's laugh back sounded good-natured.

I didn't wait long then to check on Sailor. But he looked good enough to me. That is, he was in the same room as before, sprawled on the smelly cot, and he was out of it, but he was breathing regularly and I couldn't see anything particularly worse about his condition. In fact, he was actually less dead than he usually got. When I pushed at him, there was some life in response. His body jerked and a slurry arm pushed back in protest.

The only thing was his color. It was a little more

yellowish than gray, but it might have been the light slanting in from the hall. I'd left the door open to see.

Anyway, he was all right as far as I could tell, and the way he stirred, in another hour he'd be up and returned. Pauline didn't have to be concerned and I could go back to the kitchen and finish my sandwich.

It either happenns or it doesn't, Sailor said, and you forget it. There's no such thing as nearly.

I was in the kitchen again eating my sandwich when Rita came in. I'd seen her before in a ratty robe and woolly socks, looking sad, with circles under her eyes, but this time she was completely different and I hardly knew who she was. Her face was fixed and her hair was curly and she was wearing a nice dress. She looked perky and pretty, and instead of dragging her feet, her walk was snappy, in high heels, clickity-click.

"Hi," she said, passing me brightly.

"Hullo," I said, my mouth stuffed with baloney.

She poured herself a glass of organge juice and gave me a look that seemed pointed. She was standing with one hip cocked, the glass held in both hands to her lips. But she wasn't sipping. Her tongue tip was simply licking the rim delicately and she was looking at me over the glass, her chin tucked.

"I've seen you before," she said.

"I was here yesterday, first time." I was trying to swallow.

"You waitin'?" Faintly smiling, maybe coy.

"Yeh. I'm waiting for Sailor."

"Sailor?"

"He's still sleeping."

"Oh, him—" She took a sip and licked her lips, her eyes still on me. "Is that all?"

"Yeh, I'm just waiting." Out of that old robe and those baggy socks, and the way she had her face fixed, it was amazing how she'd changed. She was really pretty. And not very old.

She put her glass down and, clickity-click, sashaying, she came right over and sat beside me. She pulled her chair close until her knees were against mine and she was leaning toward me, both her hands on one of my legs.

"My name's Rita." A big smile. "What's yours?"

"Bud."

"Hi."

"Hi." She was in my face, and I had to lean back.

"Whataya think?"

"About what?"

She giggled. "You want a good time?" She was moving her hand on my leg.

"I dunno." I didn't know if I should touch her back or not.

"You got the money, sugar, I got the time." She squeezed my thigh with both her hands and I almost jumped. But it was a good squeeze. "I think I'm just supposed to be waiting," I said.

"You can wait and still enjoy it, can't you?"

"I guess, maybe."

She moved her hand up and started rubbing. "Oh, oh, what's that?" Her eyes widened in mock surprise.

"What about Pauline?" I said.

"What about her?"

"Well—" I didn't know how to put it. "I think I kinda like Pauline."

Her face pulled back a little. "You do?" But she kept rubbing. She wasn't put off.

"I don't want to hurt your feelings."

"You don't. But this is her day with one of her regulars. She ain't gonna have time." She looked down where she was massaging and gave a little shiver. "This makes me hotter'n a firecracker, don't it you?"

I didn't have to answer. I could feel a tingle and I was hardening.

"Don'tcha like me?" she asked.

"Sure—but I like Pauline too."

"But you haven't tried me yet, have you? I'm hotter'n Pauline, and I mean hotter, real hot." She closed her eyes and sucked in her breath, feeling something.

I didn't know why I had desired Pauline. Rita was prettier and she was exciting me. Pauline's appeal, I realize now, was partly a mother's. Her big body was warm and earthy. I had wanted her big arms to enfold me, to smother my face in her breasts. I'd missed that in my life.

But Rita had me now. She had me in her hands. I reached for the space between her legs.

Just as I touched, she stopped me. "You got the money?"

"I got some."

"Ten dollars?"

"Yeh, I got that."

She stood and pulled me up with my hand. "C'mon."

"I dunno, maybe—" I wasn't that sure. Standing up was embarrassing.

Her hand went down to my bulge and patted affectionately. "You stop now, we're gonna waste that." She leaned into me and pressed against me with her breasts. "Relax, sugar, I'm gonna blow your mind."

All she had to do then was lead me.

Inside the first room down the hall, after closing

the door, she held out her hand and wiggled her fingers. "Ten dollars." Her mood had changed, and she was all business now.

I had lost my hard, but I fished in my pocket and gave her the money. She turned away to stuff the bill in her dress. Then, not wasting time, she turned back around, reached down and unzipped me. I might have half stepped back, it was so sudden, but she held me by the belt with one hand and examined me with the other, with only her fingertips touching. I tried not to move. She was frowning, looking closely, then I was skinned back and milked and when nothing dripped out, I must've passed.

"Okay," she said, "you can drop your pants. Leave your shirt on."

I unbuckled and let my pants fall. She raised her dress above her hips and lay back on the bed.

I stood, my pants around my ankles.

"C'mon," she said, "let's go." She had her knees up and her legs spread, and she had me sighted between her knees.

I started to step out of my pants. "No, no, just like that," she said. "C'mon."

I was hobbled, but I managed to get on the bed and between her legs, and I was braced on my arms when my shirttail got in the way. I tried to pull it up, but I was off balance and fumbling.

"Here." She jerked the shirt up for me and reached down to stick me in, but I was soft and wouldn't go, only a little, and that kept slipping out.

She was pushing up and trying to help. "Do it," she said, "get in there."

"I'm trying."

"Then do it, hurry up."

She kept me from her breasts, and when I tried to kiss her, she turned her head.

"C'mon, c'mon," she kept saying, "hurry it up."

All the time she had one hand down in between, working on me, and before I knew it, still soft and limber, and without a spark of sensation, I came.

She pushed me off immediately and got up, Then, with her dress held up around her waist, she went to the corner, squatted over a pan of water, dipped down, and gave herself a splashy wash.

I stood from the bed and she gave me a quick wipe with a wet rag.

I pulled up my pants. "That it?"

She held the door open. "That's it."

I walked back to the kitchen to wait for Sailor, and Rita moved into the front room to wait for another customer.

•   •   •

Sailor, of course, made it. Again, at first, he was weak and trembling and shambling, but he came into the kitchen under his own power. He seemed to barely notice me and I waited while he had coffee, spilling the first cup with shaky hands.

We didn't talk, except once I said, "You know something, you might oughta quit drinking so much." It was the first time I'd ever said that.

He raised his head slowly and looked at me a long time. Finally he said, "You leaving or staying?"

"I'm just going back with you to pick up my stuff."

He nodded.

"But you oughta quit drinking," I said.

"Yeh." Both hands were around his cup as if holding it down on the table. "Yeh, right now I'd agree."

A little later we collected Judy and Mawd and started riding them bareback along the highway to camp. Their wide backs were straight and hard, but their walk was an easy and graceful rhythm at a human pace.

The traffic was zooming by and I began to notice old pickups. I could imagine the Cranes coming up behind as fast as they could and purposely sideswiping us.

"Let's get off the highway," I said, "cut across country."

"That's harder." Sailor was slumped over Judy with his eyes closed.

"I don't like all the traffic. We could get hit."

"Never have."

"Sailor, c'mon—"

He gave me a look. "What's the problem?"

"The Cranes could come along. They got a pickup."

He waited.

"They tried to jump me this morning," I said. "I busted Spoon's nose again, and he's crazy."

"You bust him good?"

"Pretty good."

"But you didn't finish him."

"Collard and Ham jumped in. It was in town." Then I thought. "Besides, you didn't finish him either."

Sailor didn't like me saying that, but he didn't reply.

"I'm telling you," I said, "we better get off this highway."

We rode awhile, then Sailor squared his shoulders. "All right, c'mon, cross-country."

We turned our mules off the shoulder and into the woods and soon the sounds of cars and trucks faded behind us. The sounds of nature took over and we maneuvered through the trees peacefully.

We stopped once for Sailor to relieve himself. As always, it took him some time, and this time, it seemed, even longer than usual. I didn't watch, but I heard him straining.

When we started on, I guess my eyes turned. I wasn't trying to see, but I glimpsed a flash of color through the leaves where he had been, a splash of red soaked in the ground.

Sailor's face was definitely drawn.

That night he was quiet by the fire and staring at his hands. We'd cooked a pot of beans and corn pone, but he ate very little. The fire was dry cedar, popping sparks, and when one pop landed on his sleeve, he took no notice. The spark burned a hole in his shirt before I could reach and brush it away.

"Watch the sparks," I said.

He didn't move and kept staring at his hands.

I felt a chill at my back. It was his body, his hands and face, but Sailor wasn't there. For the first time I felt what it would be like without him, without his life in mine. Before, in my mind, I could go off, but Sailor would still be there. I would have that knowledge and feel it. But if he died on me, he would be nowhere. There'd be an empty place where I expected something. There'd be a dead space and his presence would be gone entirely. It gave me a strange sensation.

"A lot of things—" The words were hardly spoken. His voice was in the fire, his face still in a trance.

He left it there.

I finally asked, "What things?"

He put his hands together slowly and squinted his eyes. "A lot of things I never got around to telling you, I guess I should've." The words faded.

"Like what?"

He shifted a little and sniffed. "Just some things. Doesn't matter now."

"You can tell me."

He turned his head. "I'd just be talking—no, the way it was is the way it was." He was rubbing his palms, coming back to his natural self. "You don't need to know. It wouldn't help you, and I'd just be talking to clear my conscience." He glanced at me furtively.

But he was going to tell me, I could see that, and he might have wanted me to say it'd be okay, to make it easier, but I didn't. He'd never made it easy for me.

He went on. "You see, the trick is to live without remorse and keep yourself sane—but some things stay with you. These tattoos—" He pulled back his sleeve and showed them. "They're permanent, like everything that happens to you, that you do—What you do stays with you, you see—" He was struggling in his mind, trying to lead up to what he wanted to say, which was his way, and it always made me restless.

I interrupted. "Sailor, c'mon—"

He poked at the fire with a stick. "I probably should've left you at the Claytons'. I didn't have to come back for you."

The end of the stick caught fire, and he watched it burn. Then speaking to the stick, he said, "I should've married your mother."

That was it, and for a moment I couldn't understand why that had to be hard for him. The word "bastard" crossed my mind, but it didn't strike me with any particular effect, except it seemed so weightless. I didn't feel in the least surprised or taken back.

"But you didn't," I said.

"No—" he said softly, "I didn't."

"But it was okay with her."

"It made it hard for her."

"She went with you, though, against her family."

"She wanted to."

"Then you felt cooped-up and started running around."

"Yeh—something like that."

"And you weren't there when she had me."

"No." He dropped the burning stick in the fire, and the part he'd held blazed. "But I could've been."

"So she died."

"She bled to death on her own—the Claytons found her." He hung his head. "They said she was still holding you."

I could see myself newborn, splotchy red and slick as an otter, crying against a cold body, a dead stiff arm crooked around me, Murph's and Mattie's eyes looking down. We were on an Indian blanket on the floor.

Some time went by in silence. Judy and Mawd were asleep on their feet in the trees. The fire died down to coals and the night owls came out.

Sailor stood up and leaned over to flex his knees, to unkink them. "'Bout that time," he said, meaning to turn in.

"And the gold," I said. "You never struck it rich, did you?"

"I used to make up those stories when you were little, remember? About gold in the Amazon, in the headwaters of the Orinoco, and all the headhunters around. You used to like to hear 'em."

"But you kept on. You keep looking for gold in the rocks, all the time."

"You used to help me."

"So you lied."

"They were just stories, Bud. You used to believe in 'em. You wanted me to tell you."

"But you kept on."

"I was just foolin'." He paused. "I guess I didn't notice, you grew up on me."

"I guess I did."

"Yeah—you did."

His tone made me look up, and his eyes were sad. I had to look away.

"You should've married her," I said.

My mother alone—that started me, I think, and brought the others to mind, one after another—Hominy, Lew, Sailor, Pauline, Stella, Rita, the people on the phone— all alone. And nobody was touching. It was like we all had a space around us and were all isolated in some kind of invisible shell. The world around was busy with life, with animals and birds interwoven. That life was meshed together in the trees, but people were alone and separate.

I knew I was only seeing a certain view, but I couldn't change it or turn it off.

Sailor was lying still and breathing quietly, and I knew he was awake—his mind was in the air too. Our bedrolls were not that far apart.

I whispered, "Sailor—"

He grunted.

"I can't sleep—nobody fits."

"Where?"

"Together—everybody's alone."

"Go to sleep."

"But doesn't anybody fit?"

A moment. Then, "Some say they do."

"Yeh, but do they?"

"They might if they think they do. You can't rule it out."

"Yeh, but everybody I know, it just seems like they're alone and they don't fit."

"Go to sleep."

"Well, am I right, or what?"

"That's up to you to figure."

"Just tell me."

"I dunno—I've never known myself."

He'd lifted me above his head and I was looking down at his red and blue tattoos. "Who're you?" I said. His eyes widened. "Who'm I?" He hefted me higher. "Who'm I, the kid says!" He was laughing and I was afraid he was going to throw me away.

We worked the next day, and because I felt it would be the last logging I'd ever do, I put my back into it. The sweat rolled and it felt good. I wanted every stroke to count and I wanted to feel every bite I took with the ax. To make it final. To say good-bye and mean it. I tried to wear myself out.

But Sailor was different. His swing was still long. It was still curved and smooth and he had that natural stance, but the real flow was missing. The power was gone. He chopped more slowly, deliberately, and for the first time I kept up.

Once he looked at me ahead of him and he tried to smile, but his mouth was crooked, and the smile failed at the corners. There was a dull bleakness in his eyes.

And once he slipped. One knee went to the ground,

and instead of getting up, he stayed on the knee and pretended to rest.

I asked, "You tired?"

"Maybe. Not much."

"You don't look too hot."

"I've felt worse."

"Let's quit."

He got to his feet and I was surprised he agreed. "Yeh, we've done enough. Let's quit."

Sailor lay in camp while I finished the afternoon planting the Kentucky Wonders I'd swiped from the hardware store. I remembered the package was still in my pocket, and if I wouldn't be around, I could still plant them and imagine them growing. Maybe somebody would find them and have a nice meal. They wouldn't have to string them, and they could have fresh green beans with chunks of ham boiling in a pot. I made two long rows beside the logging trail.

Night again. The fire. Yams baking in the coals. The corned beef already fried and waiting. Sailor sitting across the little flames, looking at his hands, his eyes hooded in shadows.

Judy and Mawd were in their regular night place off to the side, and I started watching them. They had that dreamy way they liked to stand and nuzzle each other and I enjoyed watching them. I liked their smells in the air and the way they moved so lazily. They could look so calm and peaceful. But it was strength at rest. When they needed to, when they knew you wanted them to, they could bunch that strength in an instant and explode with power. Hitched to timber, they could throw themselves against that weight and snap the hauling chain like a whip. The big iron links would be stretched taut, vibrating. The timber would come off the ground.

So it was that hidden power in them too, beneath their quiet ways. I was going to miss feeling that. And the fire in the open. It seemed I had sat around that same everlasting flame my whole life, listening to the sounds in the trees—

But it was a light feeling, not bad, and I didn't get sentimental.

Sailor didn't eat.

"Not hungry," he said.

"How come?"

He didn't answer.

"Good yams," I said.

He still didn't answer. His eyes were flickering in the firelight. Yellowish and white.

I took a breath. "You're dying, aren't you?"

"Dying?" He almost smiled. "That's the last thing I'm gonna do."

"You can tell me."

"You trying to get messy?"

"No, not especially."

"Then don't— Look, when I get ready to bow out, I'll let you know, okay?"

"Okay."

I let it drop. His jaw was set.

Later we were in our bedrolls and I couldn't sleep.

"I don't guess there's anything you forgot to tell me," I said.

"Like what?"

"Like you didn't get around to, and you should've, like you said."

Silence. Then, "I guess not."

"Okay." I rolled over and closed my eyes. "G'night."

"G'night."

Then sometime in the night I was falling asleep and barely heard. It might have been a dream. But it was Sailor's voice in the dark, in the quiet.

"One thing," he said, "I want you to know—I loved your mother."

I was driving. Sailor was on the buckboard beside me and we were going to town. My extra clothes and bedroll and ax were loaded behind. I'd offered to leave my ax, but Sailor didn't need it. If I had no use for it again, he said, I could sell it. A good used ax like that would be worth a few dollars.

I focused on the backs of Judy and Mawd and let them go at their own pace, and the wagon seemed to creep along. Cars whizzed by and trucks swamped us in their wake, and I felt like something from out of the past coming for the first time into a modern world. It was a feeling I'd had before, and when we got to town I knew the traffic would stack up behind us, horns would honk, and people would gawk.

But soon I'd be free of that, of being some kind of spectacle, and I was never again going to ride in a wagon that stayed in the past.

I fixed my eyes straight ahead where the highway traveled out of sight beyond Judy and Mawd. Only their ears stuck up into my line of vision, and only occasionally was I aware of any sound around me, of the axles creaking or any wheels turning at all.

6

The pulling contest booth at the fair grounds was set up behind the rodeo pens and that's where you had to go to sign up. Which we did. Sailor paid the ten-dollar entrance fee and they gave us a number. The next morning they'd draw the numbers from a box and announce the pulling positions. Actually, in the end, it wouldn't matter what position you were in. The contest was round robin, so they could have more easily placed the teams in order of entry. But they did it by the numbers, the way things are supposed to be officially.

Around the corner of the pens, not far from the contest booth, the men who'd entered teams and some others were gathered in a group. They were talking about the different teams and making bets and we joined in.

Chubb, from the sawmill, was in the center and I was surprised to see him holding the bets and setting the odds. At least, on one particular team he was offering two-to-one odds, but there were no takers.

"The Mount Vernon team?" someone said. "No way."

"C'mon, two-to-one," Chubb said. "That's fair."

"Go find yourself another sucker. Not me."

Chubb saw me. "How 'bout you?" But before I could answer, he turned away. "Naw, I don't wanna take your money. You're too young."

Sailor asked a man next to him, "What's the deal on Mount Vernon?"

"They're big," the man said. "Special bred."

"Where've they pulled?"

"Last year at Hanksboro, they won hands down."

"Pretty easy, huh?"

"Wasn't even a contest."

"Where else they pulled?"

"That was it, first and only time out—but you shoulda seen 'em."

"Good, huh?"

"Big. Ain't nothing around here gonna touch 'em."

Sailor let it go and made a few straight bets on the side, our team against someone else's, even money. Each time, Chubb was given the money to hold. I found out later, if you wanted to bet horse races or ball games around the country, Chubb was the man for that too.

I didn't see how much Sailor bet, but I think it was only a ten or a twenty here and there, not a lot.

He asked the first man again, "That Mount Vernon pair, they a working team too?"

"Oh, no, hell, you kiddin'? They're too valuable."

"A showboat team."

"You ain't seen 'em."

"Well, I'll tell you this, they're not a working team, they're gonna be soft, cow pasture mules."

"Shit, man, you ain't seen 'em."

"But they're still mules, right?"

"They're fuckin' giants!"

"They still walk on four legs and shit on the ground. I don't care how big they are, if they've never been worked, they're gonna be soft. They're gonna play out. I got a team that can take 'em."

"Wanna put your money where your mouth is?" Chubb had been listening and now he was right there.

Sailor blinked and pretended to back off. But I knew him. "I dunno," he said. "How much you giving?"

"Two-to-one."

"Is that all?"

"Is that all? Where else you gettin' two-to-one?"

"And where else you gettin' any takers?"

Chubb grinned and his Oriental eyes were slits. "Aw, c'mon, Sailor, two-to-one's double, more than fair."

"Not from what I hear, and I don't see anybody else taking you up. Two big ol' Mount Vernon mules, special bred? You're being chintzy, Chubb. C'mon—"

"Whataya want then?"

"Gimme four-to-one."

"You're outta your mind, four-to-one!"

They dickered, and the crowd looked on.

Finally Sailor got three-to-one, handed over a hundred dollars, and Chubb put it in the book. At those odds I was tempted to bet my fifty-dollar nest egg, but I held back. A bet was still a chance and anything special bred might be something I didn't know.

I still felt Judy and Mawd could win. I had faith in them. But *what if* was in my mind too. *What if*, with me, was nearly always hanging around. The same with *what next*. I could never see that coming, except in a flash. And this time, as usual, I had no flash. So I didn't bet.

The Cranes happened then, Spoon, Collard, and Ham. While the betting was going on, they had eased into the crowd and stood back. I hadn't noticed. But just as the betting ended and we were about to leave, Spoon stepped forward. "Wanna bet?"

I immediately braced and felt my skin crawl. He was coming after me, I thought. He's here to get me. And it's going to be now. I had a sudden feeling of fear and weakness. But it has to be, I thought, and at the same time, why? Why didn't he just go away?—All of that in an instant. And revulsion too. I wouldn't have said that word then, but that's what I felt, a revulsion for his ratlike meanness, the smell of him, the scrawny inbred thing he was.

But he ignored me. He was talking to Sailor.

"Wanna bet, I'll betcha," he said. He had a dirty tape across his nose and his nostrils were clotted with black blood. Collard and Ham stood behind him like two morons.

"I'm through betting," Sailor said. But he and Spoon were the center now. The crowd was watching.

1 6 9

"That's too bad," Spoon said. "I was kinda lookin'
to make a bet with you." He had his hands slouched in
his pockets, his bent neck thrust forward.

"Like what?"

"Ya know, I lost me a hun'erd dollars oncet on a
pair of mules, jis' like you got—I was kinda hopin' to
make that back." He knew he had the attention of the
crowd and he was playing to it.

Sailor shrugged him. "Nah, I've already bet my
money."

"Yeh, but you can still come up with something
can'tcha?"

"My money's bet." Sailor was ready to turn away.

"What about your mules? They're worth something, ain't they?" Spoon's nose was dripping a yellow
stream now that slowly oozed around his split lip. The
bruises under his eyes were tinged greenish at the
edges.

Sailor was turning, but Spoon stopped him. "I'll
make you a little bet, my money against your mules,
they don't win." He waited with his mouth open, his
tongue lolled.

Sailor narrowed his eyes. "How much?"

Spoon leaned back arrogantly. "Well, now—like I
said, I lost a hun'erd dollars oncet on a pair of mules
jis' like them you got, but I wouldn't ask *you* to put up
no fine set of mules like that for no measly hun'erd
bucks. Couldn't expect ya to, could I? But I got five
hun'erd that says you can't win and you're gonna lose
your ass." He thrust his neck out again.

Sailor's face hardened. "Where's your money?"

"Right here in my pocket."

"Get it out, sonofabitch, you're on."

Spoon leered, pulled out a handful of bills and

started counting. "And I didn't steal this neither," he said.

Chubb nudged Sailor's elbow and pulled him a little sideways and whispered, "Sailor, you might not oughta do this—"

"I'm doing it."

"Now, wait a minute, you're betting your team you can win the whole contest. You haven't seen that Mount Vernon team yet."

"I bet you, didn't I?"

"Yeah, but just a hundred, not your team. That's part of your livelihood."

"I'm not gonna lose."

"Sailor, I'm advising ya—"

"You don't have to."

"Okay, it's your team."

Judy and Mawd.

Sailor wrote a note signing over the mules to Spoon if he lost, and Chubb was given the note and cash to hold.

Chubb looked at me as if to say he'd tried and he was sorry.

Spoon and his brothers went through the crowd, grinning and twisting their asses as if they knew something we didn't, as if they'd already won. It was insulting and my revulsion for them rose again.

At the corner of the pens Spoon turned and looked back directly at me. He was sneering through the dirty tape across his nose, and then he raised his arm and whipped me the finger.

"You bastard!" I yelled. And I started for him as he turned his back and disappeared behind the pens.

But Sailor grabbed my shoulder and held me. "Let it go."

"The bastard!"

"Forget it."

"He's a coward!"

"It's all right, we'll get 'em tomorrow."

I wasn't finished, but some of the men were grinning at me, the way I was acting, and I clamped my mouth.

"Don't worry." Sailor patted my shoulder. "We'll show 'em tomorrow."

"We better." The heat stayed in me a while longer, and then I was all right. It would be all right.

Tomorrow, I thought. Judy and Mawd were bet against five hundred dollars and they were going against a team supposedly unbeatable, but I wasn't worried. That Mount Vernon team could be big, they could be specially bred, but they had never worked and that's what counted. Judy and Mawd had worked their whole lives harder than anyone.

The drugstore next. I was going to walk by, make a casual pass. Then, if it felt right, maybe I'd stop in. It had been two days.

But Hominy wasn't there.

I asked the woman behind the cash register.

"Not here," the woman said.

"Her day off?"

"She's not working here anymore."

"She's not?" A jolt, a surprise. "How come?"

"I wouldn't know."

"She just quit, or what?"

"You'd have to ask her." Prim lips, an enemy mouth.

I walked out slowly, thinking.

She could already be packed and gone—that's what I was thinking, but I had to find out, and I started walking to her house.

Along the way I felt the cars passing, moving on. The street was paved.

I saw myself getting left behind.

You know, when you're walking, you're not traveling. Not really moving. You're getting passed by cars going places and they don't care, their way is paved. But you're walking. A car comes along, and then it's gone, and you're still there, still nowhere.

Behind my back, it seemed, the world had paved itself for cars and left me out.

In my mind, a green car zoomed by with the ghost of two heads behind the wheel and I was left in a swirl beside the road. Ridiculously, I raised my hand and waved.

The worst feeling then was walking the empty road.

"She says she don't wanna see you." Hominy's landlady had finally come to the back door after I'd knocked several times. She was a small woman with a big nose.

"Tell her I need to talk to her, it's important."

"She told me to tell you to go away."

"Tell her just for a minute. There's something I need to tell her."

The woman made a face and went back in the house. I could see her in the hall at Hominy's door. Then she went on into the front of the house and Hominy came out.

She stopped at the screen door and looked down at

me on the steps. I expected to see her upset, but she looked normal. "Okay," she said, "you got something to tell me."

"Yeah—" I couldn't think.

"Well?" She leaned against the door frame. "What is it? I'm waiting."

I smiled. "I'm back."

"I didn't know you were gone."

"I've been gone two days. You said you needed some time—"

"Is that what you've got to tell me?" She pushed from the frame impatiently.

"Wait, I went by the drugstore. They said you're not working there anymore."

"Well, ain't you Mr. Know-it-all. You find out everything."

"I thought you needed to work, to save some money."

"I got fired."

"How come?"

She lowered her head and shook it.

I opened the screen door. "C'mon, talk to me—just for a minute. You gotta tell me what happened."

"Whataya wanna know for? Whata you care?"

"I just do."

She came out with a careless toss of her head and we sat together on the back steps. It was like the first time except now it was daylight. She sat with her knees up and she was wearing her jeans and red shirt.

"They accused me of stealing. They were missing things outta Cosmetics and they accused me of sneaking 'em."

"But you didn't."

"Mr. Reedy called me back in his office and tried

to get me to admit it, and I told him it wasn't me, I didn't do it, but he wouldn't believe me."

I was more aware than ever now of her dark eyelashes and red lips. There was a faintly violet shadow also above her eyes. "He should've had proof," I said.

"He didn't have nothing—I mean, anything." She corrected herself. "He just said he knew."

"I think they have to catch a person stealing or they can't do anything."

"Well, they didn't catch nobody. They couldn't prove nothing." Then she corrected herself again. "I mean, anybody, anything." She was bound and determined to get those double negatives.

"If he couldn't prove it, he shouldn't have fired you. I don't think that's right."

"Yeh, well, I think he just wanted to get rid of me. I think he heard things about me." She rested her head on her arms across her knees.

"What things?"

"You know—I think everybody knows now." Her voice was almost too soft to hear.

I didn't know what to say.

With her head still down, she murmured, "Who did you tell?"

"Nobody. I didn't tell."

It was a hard moment and she was absolutely still.

"I wouldn't tell," I said. "Honest."

"Well—" She kept her face hidden in her arms. "I see people looking at me now—I took three baths today."

"Three?" But not real baths, I thought.

"I get out of the tub, I still feel dirty."

"But you're not."

"I don't know what." A small shiver went through her shoulders.

I reached to touch her, to pet her, and she jerked away. "Don't touch me."

I stuffed my hands between my legs. "I'm sorry."

She finally raised her head, but she didn't look at me. She looked in the distance across the yard. "Why'd you have to sneak around?"

"I didn't mean to."

"I thought you were going to be somebody I could like."

"I'm sorry, I really am."

"I can't even look at you now."

"I wish you could."

For a moment that was it.

Then I thought. "Hey, guess what?" She didn't turn, and I went on. "My face is growing back, I can almost see it in the mirror now."

"I don't like you looking at me either." Dully.

"Hominy—"

"Why don't you just leave? Why'd you have to come around? I was doing just fine."

"The first time I saw you—"

"And don't gimme that. I don't want to hear that stuff." A color had risen in her cheeks.

"Just the same—"

"I told you, I don't want to hear it. I don't like you."

"Or maybe you don't like yourself."

She turned now and blinked. "Whataya mean?"

"I just said that."

"Well, I do, I like myself just fine."

"I didn't mean it, I just said it."

"I like myself." More color rising, angrily.

"Okay—"

"You're the one that don't like yourself. How could you? Look at your face."

I was a plain mask again with two cut-out holes for eyes. "You can get back at me if you want to," I said. "I never said I was handsome."

"Don't worry, you ain't." She turned back.

Again we sat.

But it didn't last long. Her feelings eased and she spoke softly. "I'm sorry. It ain't you—but I gotta go somewhere now. I gotta move on."

"Where?"

She was rubbing her knees, looking down. "I dunno. I can't get a job now. They'll tell everybody they fired me for stealing." She pushed at her knees. "And I know who it was too."

"Who?"

"The cashier, ol' Wanda. She was always walking over to Cosmetics, foolin' around. I saw her sneak a lipstick once. Acted like she dropped it, then bent over and stuck it in her shoe. She wears those big ol' slippers all the time 'cause she's got flat feet, it hurts her to stand."

"You should've told."

"You mean tattled."

"Well, not that. But you didn't have to take the blame."

"Yeh. Well, like I said—" She didn't finish, that they'd heard things, that they wanted to fire her anyway. She shook her head. "I gotta go someplace I can get work, where they don't know me."

"You were going to save some money to go on."

"Well, I can't now."

"So how're you going?"

"I'll just go."

"I've got fifty dollars."

"That's yours."

"But you can have it. I'll loan it to you."

"And then what?"

I hesitated. "I want to go with you."

She turned away again. "I told you, the way every-thing is, I gotta forget. I don't want to remember—and you'd just keep reminding me."

"I wouldn't."

"You remind me just sitting here."

"I'm not trying to."

"But you do—" She clenched her jaw. "All right, so it's me and not you. What's the difference? I don't wanna keep seeing it!"

Her voice had risen, and now there was a halt. We were both stopped. Knowing what I did about her made me the wrong thing, but there was still some-thing between us and it seemed we both knew it. I sensed that, but it wasn't enough.

"I see you looking at me," she said. "I know what you think."

"Not that."

"Yeah, you do." She sighed. "Anyway, I just made up my mind. I'm gonna leave Sunday."

"This Sunday?" It was so sudden.

"That's when Darryl goes back to his base, to Fort Hood."

"Fort Hood," I repeated.

"That's down in Texas."

"So you like him?" I felt shrunken.

"I never said that." She stood up.

"But you're going with him."

"Yeah—" I knew what she was going to say next, and she did. "He's got a car."

A green car, I thought, spinning wheels in the gravel.

"It's a ride to Dallas," she said.

She opened the screen door and stepped onto the porch.

I stood and felt hollow.

She was hesitating. "Look," she said, "I know you tried to be nice—" Her voice faltered.

"What about money?" I said.

"I can do without. I can still make it."

"It'd be easier, though, if you had some."

"Just the same, I got a ride, I'm going."

"To Dallas."

"To where nobody knows me—I can start over." She turned quickly and hurried on into the house.

—where nobody knows me, she'd said, but they think I'm nice and they like me and everywhere I go, I'm smiling—

"I don't know about that," I said, "I don't think people smile all the time."

But I didn't say it loud. I was talking to the screen.

·   ·   ·

It seemed a connection inside me had sprung. I could feel the seepage and a pressure escaping my body.

Sunday was another day, but I could see it coming. I had planned to be with her. I'd found her and made plans. Of course, there'd never been an understanding. It had all been in my head, a hope, what I wanted. I could reason that. But, still, when she left, I'd feel deserted.

It was going to be me in town with nobody. And for the first time, for real, just me.

I marched back to the fair grounds and found Chubb and bet my fifty against the supposedly great Mount Vernon team.

Chubb gave me three-to-one, but he kept asking me if I was sure, if I knew what I was doing, and I kept telling him I did.

Then it was Pauline's. I might've had some downhill instinct, and I wanted to slide as far as I could, but people were in for the festival, and when I walked in and saw eight men waiting in line, I turned around and left.

The Belvedere next.

Lew was fussing with boxes, getting things together to take to his stand at the festival, the little projects he'd turned into objects to sell.

He tried to show me. "Here's the nest you saw," he said, "but you didn't see the bird I finished. Look."

I was walking by and I didn't want to look.

"What's the matter?" he said, his eyes enlarged.

I didn't answer.

I locked my door and lay down on the bed and stared at the ceiling. A prisoner in a cell. That's the way it was. You're alone in this world and you find it out sooner or later, you might as well face it.

"Bud, you let your feelings get in the way."
"I can't help what I feel."
"Then you can't help nothing."

A tap on the door and Lew's whispery worried voice. "Bud—are you all right?"

"Leave me alone."

"Is there anything I can do?"

"No."

"Are you sure?"

"Get the hell away from my door!"

His footsteps ticked away, sticking to the linoleum.

After you've lived awhile, you know how it is. You've seen the plain waste of good things. The wayside is heaped with the rusty wrecks of old heartbreaks. The litter of hurt is commonplace. All the paths you've crossed are strewn with emotional rubble, and you've seen in the wind the scraps and pieces of what might have been. You know how it piles up, and after a while you can lie in the dark and stare at the ceiling forever. I've done it.

But when you're younger, it's different. On its own, the state you're in changes and you go on. You don't just keep lying there.

I finally got up and washed my face and felt better. I decided to move around and left by the alley through the back door.

It was early night and the stars were out. A clear fresh feel was in the air and I could smell the leaves in the trees.

I went to the pasture where we'd left Judy and Mawd and the wagon, and that was a peaceful place. The field was smoothly grassed and the stream was running quietly, racing its channel with hardly a ripple. A raccoon appeared and washed its hands but made no sound. Its face was masked and then it was gone. Fireflies winked in a calm space.

Judy and Mawd were standing asleep and I let

them stand. The wagon was at rest too, with its long tongue out to the ground. My bedroll and clothes and ax were still in it and I might have taken them back to my room then, but I didn't. The ax blade I'd kept sharpened shone in the dark wagon like a sliver of moon.

Then music came floating with a beat in the air and I was drawn to that.

It was called a street dance, to start the festival, but it was really a parking lot dance at the fair grounds. Hay bales had been set around the perimeter and a band played from a stand at one end. There was a beer concession in back, but people also brought their own in coolers, so it was easy. Little kids were playing and running around on their own too, and I liked that, that kids could belong.

I sat on a hay bale at one end and watched and it was a good crowd. For every type dance there were at least a dozen different dancing styles, couples who had their own method for following the music. And some with no method at all, but that didn't stop them.

I had fun spotting the individual types and I guess on any dance floor you can find them—the big dippers and prancers, the bulldozers, the spiders and creepers, the skaters and all kinds, all moving their own way and having their own good time.

I think I like best the tilt-a-whirls who keep going round and round and never stop. They make you think they'll finally get dizzy and fall down, or should, but they never do. I also like the girls showing off their legs.

I made up my mind, first chance I got, I was going to take some free lessons at Arthur Murray's. At the same time, I was enjoying myself just watching.

Then I saw Hominy and Darryl standing across the lot. They looked like they'd just arrived and stopped.

All at once the crowd seemed to blur and the two of them stood out.

She was in a blue dress and very pretty. He was wearing his uniform with his cap pushed back and his tie loosened.

I felt my face changing. So that's him, I thought. He had a beer in one hand and his arm draped carelessly around Hominy's shoulders. His mouth was fixed with a sappy half grin and his uniform gave him a certain look, not exactly pressed or neat, but regular. He looked like every young soldier I've ever seen since, and you've seen his photograph on dressers. He and his buddies are horsing around some camp. They're sitting on the steps of some barracks spit-shining their boots. They're loading some army truck, marching along some dirt road, dogtags dangling from their necks. And they're all getting drunk on beer. That was him. He'd joined the army to see the world and he was standing there with Hominy as if placed by a whim. Grinning.

She was holding her elbows with her forearms across her stomach, and she made his arm on her shoulders look heavy. Her face was vacant and she was keeping her body apart from his. So she didn't like that arm on her, even casually. That was touching leading to embracing and she didn't go for that. Still, she looked so pretty.

I felt sad. She appeared closed to the music, but I wondered about her feelings. Outside, she was indifferent. But inside, what was the beat there while the band played a polka? She'd bathed three times that day. She'd washed me off in the river.

I felt the distance between us. She wanted to talk better. And do better. She wanted to learn, and somewhere down the road maybe she'd find her way and keep going. But the damage was done. She'd meet you down by the river, but don't try to kiss.

They danced and she was following, but Darryl had his own steps and they kept missing. He tried to hold her close and she kept pushing back. I could've told him, but his mouth stayed fixed in that same half grin and he didn't seem to care.

She was going through the motions but not really dancing. She kept her face turned and her body was dead to the music.

She needs to leave, I thought. She needs to start all over again. Where nobody knows.

I saw myself looking, and I saw I had been given a new face with regular features, and it was good. It was all together a sturdy face. But the expression was a little sad, a little too thoughtful.

They were standing again and I walked toward them. She saw me coming and pretended not to, but I didn't care.

I stepped close. "I just want to say good-bye."

She couldn't look at me and glanced anxiously at Darryl. I could smell her clean skin. "And good luck," I said.

Darryl moved in. "Who're you?"

"It's okay," I said. "We're just friends."

He blinked, his mouth still fixed, and Hominy looked away as if in pain.

And that's the way I left them.

I walked away feeling lonely. And yet somehow free. You're alone in this life, I thought, and that's the way it is. That's the fact of the matter and you better count on it, the miserable fact of life.

But it was also okay. Alone and free, right then, didn't feel too bad, too unbearable.

Later, of course, you learn there's no such thing as one without the other. And finally there's no such thing as either. But that comes later.

．　　．　　．

I flipped the light on in my room and saw the lump in my bed. Then I saw the tattoos on the arm sticking out.

Sailor turned his head from the covers and raised his hand against the light, squinting.

"You're not at Pauline's," I said.

"She was full up. Festival crowd." He coughed. "You mind?"

"No—" But he was on the left side. "You got my place, though. I like to sleep on that side."

He groaned and moved. "How's that?"

"Fine." I flipped off the light, pulled off my clothes, and got into the bed beside him.

We touched and he shifted farther. " 'Nough room?"

"Yeh, plenty."

"All right." He was resettling his side.

"You're turning in early," I said.

"Big day tomorrow."

But a big day had never stopped him before. "So Pauline's place was full up?" I said.

"I told you."

It felt odd being that close to him with both our bodies naked. And his body had no heat in it. Or I couldn't sense any. His breathing was rattling, straining through the thick matter in his lungs and I imagined waking up with a cold corpse lying beside me. Pauline didn't want him croaking at her place. A dead body never earned her a dime.

1 8 5

I finally asked, "Are you okay?"

"Why wouldn't I be?"

"You're breathing hard."

"I'm going to sleep."

That was all.

Sometime in the night, I felt smothered and woke with his arms around me, hugging me, but he was asleep and didn't know it. He was muttering gibberish in a dream and I had to shove hard to get free and get his sticky armpits away.

Then, for the rest of the night, I could only doze off and on. He'd never hugged me in any way before, and I felt disturbed.

He'd come back for me. I figured I owed you, he said. But he didn't have to. I was doing fine in that house, I remember. Murph and Mattie were easy and warm. We had jars of food in the cellar and a gourd dipper for water. Murph pulled the buckets brimming from the cistern and whittled sticks with a bone-handled knife. He struck matches with his thumb. Mattie spit snuff and the corners of her mouth were brown. She smelled like apples and her hands were forever dusted with flour.

Then Sailor came and took me away and we lived in the trees away from people. But you learned to take care of yourself, he said, you got to grow up naturally. Owing me, but not any favor. I loved your mother, he said. But what about me?

.   .   .

The next day the fair grounds crowded early.

By the time Sailor and I arrived with Judy and Mawd, most of the other teams were harnessed and ready to go in the field. A heightened sense of anticipation was in the air and people were already sitting in the bleachers overlooking the pulling arena.

I counted two dozen teams and the whole was a colorful sight. Most were decorated with tassels and nearly all the mules had ribbons in their reins and bells on their hames. A couple had flowers in their collars and because the teams were strangers crowded together, some were restless and snorting. They'd stamp their hooves and toss their heads and their jingling bells and trace chains would sound almost musical. A puff of wind now and then stirred their smells, but not bad.

Most of the mules also had their manes roached and a portion of their tails shaved in the contest style, but Judy and Mawd didn't. Our rigging was old and plain too, but Judy and Mawd held their heads high with their ears alert and twitching and I felt proud. When I rubbed them, I could feel the river of harmony under their smooth coats and the eagerness in their blood. They knew something was coming, and they were ready. I kept them settled, adjusting their straps and making over them in the small ways they liked. "You're the best," I told them, "the best there is." Their nostrils were like velvet.

When we got in the contest, they'd line up to my directions and Sailor would drive them with a flick of the wrist and the softest words. They'd pull with their big bodies slanting forward, their necks reaching, their legs stabbing, and they would look good, really good. They'd pull until they couldn't, and more if you asked.

The special Mount Vernon team had yet to arrive, but there was still time and Chubb wasn't concerned. "They'll be here," he said. "They like to make a show coming in at the last minute." He was walking around, greeting people, slapping backs, and laughing. You could tell he was confident his three-to-one odds were safe.

The Cranes had taken a position at the end of the field away from the general public. They were squatted on their haunches like ugly scavengers, and even in the distance I could see their faces smirking. I tried not to let it bother me, but I wanted the contest to begin, so we could hurry and win and wipe those smirks away. Spoon especially. I wanted to rid his face from my mind forever, but first I wanted to see it melt when we won.

Then a doubt entered my head. What if we didn't win? Sailor was looking bad. He'd been fine when we got up, but now I noticed him moving clumsily. One foot was sort of dragging. His body was acting funny.

When he sat for a while, he appeared off balance. I'd never seen him sit quite like that before and I thought he was going to fall over. He was tilting slowly. But he didn't fall.

He got up and went to the portable john set behind the bleachers. I saw him fumbling at the door to open it.

I waited—a long time.

When he finally came out, his face appeared stricken. He was wobbly and his shirt was sweated. There was a tremor in his hands.

I went to him. "You all right?"

"Yeh—" He wiped his face. "Stomach's a little queasy." He was trying to hide his hands.

"You better sit down."

"Yeh—for a minute." For the first time in his life he leaned on me, and I walked him to a bench. He sat down carefully, as if his legs were brittle.

"You didn't eat breakfast," I said. "You might need something on your stomach."

"Yeh—maybe."

"I'll get you a hot dog." The stand was near.

"No—I don't want anything."

"Something—"

"Nothing. Don't bother." He was leaning on his elbows, looking at the ground between his legs.

"Maybe I can do the pull by myself," I said.

He shook his head. "Takes two."

"Maybe I can find somebody to help me."

"Help you?" It slowly penetrated. It was as if he hadn't heard, but now he did. He sat up. "Whataya mean? You're helping me."

"If you can make it."

His eyes sparked. "Who said I couldn't?"

"You're sick—"

"And when I get too sick to make it, I'll let you know. Here—" He fished in his pocket with a trembling hand and came out with a dollar. "Here, go get me a Coke."

I took the dollar and walked away.

He was going to be too sick for the contest and we'd end up losing. The river rats would get Judy and Mawd because he'd bet them, and he always lost when he gambled because he didn't care. He was a stupid drunk and a waste—that was part of my feelings. But another part of me felt for him too. He was sick, and I wanted to help him. If he'd just tell me, but he never asked for help. Still, maybe I could let him know I was sorry. We'd shared a life. That was in me too.

But it was also sentimental stuff and I shut it off. He's sick, I thought, leave it at that.

I saw Lew's table not far from the drink stand. It was in a line with others outside the trade building and the row looked like a small flea market. All the tables were stacked with worthless glassware and little pieces of junk and simple handcrafted objects. Lew's feathered bird was on its nest in the middle of his table, and a sign on a stick said "Lew's Creations." Some woman was looking at his things, and I could almost hear him saying, "You see, I get my ideas from my materials. Now, this one, for instance—" He was smiling, and his magnified eyes appeared set out in front of his head. He'd be there all day long with people stopping and looking at his table and whether he sold anything or not, he'd be happy as a tick.

He saw me and waved but I pretended not to notice.

Sailor drank the Coke slowly and acted better. His hands steadied, and some color came back into his face. But he was still pretty weak.

The contest was going to start in another fifteen minutes. The pulling positions had been announced, and we were number ten. The Mount Vernon team was number nine, just ahead of us, but they had yet to arrive, and I started hoping they wouldn't. Maybe we could win by default. Otherwise, Sailor might not be strong enough—

Suddenly the crowd around quieted. A big blue trailer was stopping in the middle of the field and two men in blue jackets were getting out.

"Mount Vernon," someone said.

The two men lowered the tailgate as a ramp from the trailer to the ground. The side of the trailer moved as if a great weight inside had been tilted, but nothing could be seen.

Then someone near me gasped. "Good Gawd!"

Two huge red mules came backing down the ramp and a murmur of awe lifted from the crowd.

I felt stunned.

Those two mules were giants. They were also sleek and glossy and absolutely beautiful. They wheeled to the ground, high-stepping. Their hames shone with chrome, and triangles of metal gleamed in their harnesses. Their collars were studded with twinkling spikes, and their hooves were polished. They were steel shod, and high above their heads, like two battle flags, two purple plumes fluttered in the air.

Their handlers gave them directions to turn and they obeyed instantly. Their muscles bulged and rippled and they obviously had the power to match their size. They were in perfect condition, and although tremendously large, they moved with airy grace. It seemed nearly magical. They were nothing less than brilliant and a poorer team standing near appeared dwarfed.

The crowd applauded. Chubb was beaming, and farther away, the Cranes were crowing.

Sailor was standing beside me now, and we simply looked at each other, empty-handed.

A bell somewhere was ringing the start of the pull.

7

The first round of pulling was only a kind of parade.
The sled was purposely loaded light to give all the
teams an easy time and a chance to show themselves at
least once.

Each team in turn was trotted around the field
with its driver reining behind. Then it was hitched to
the sled by a helper and lined straight, and after they
made their pull, after the string behind paid out its
length ten feet and jerked the peg from the ground, the
teams were unhitched and trotted off, and the crowd
would give each a nice little round of applause.

Sailor found some strength and we made the first pull the same as the others without any trouble. Judy and Mawd knew what they were there for, and as soon as I hitched them, without needing to be lined up and without any signal from Sailor, they made their own start and the light load for only ten feet gave them no strain.

But the big red Mount Vernon team stole the show. They came out dashing with their bright plumes streaming and their harnesses gleaming, and instead of simply backing, they whirled in reverse at the sled, froze for the quick hitch with their haunches quivering, and then shot forward. It seemed they leaped the ten feet and the snappy blue-coated handlers weren't driving them so much as holding them in check.

They were an awesome sight and they brought the crowd to its feet, cheering.

In a morbid sort of way I was awed too, but I was trying not to see ahead or consider anything but the next round, the simplest next step. Sailor was also keeping his face set. It seemed what was happening was *out there*, beyond me, and if I didn't think it mattered, maybe it wouldn't. Just keep going, I thought. And don't look around. I knew the Cranes were *out there*, watching gleefully, and I didn't need to see that either.

A tractor was pulling the sled back to the starting place each time and the second round was much like the first. The sled wasn't loaded much more heavily, and every team had another easy pull. Sailor and I again went through the motions, but this time, afterward, he sat down.

Then the weight for the sled was increased quite a bit for the third round, and again for the fourth, and different teams failed. It was a pull now, but Judy and

Mawd made it easily both these rounds with their first try. And, of course, the big reds made it look like play. The blue coats had them prancing and tossing their purple plumes. Their glittering harnesses made them look rich.

As the teams dropped out of the contest, the ones hitting their limit would fishtail, bump against each other, and lose their momentum. The driver would have to realign them, and after a final third try that was again too much, some mules were simply hanging in their straps with their chests to the ground and their legs useless behind them. They'd hang there exhausted and look pitiful.

Looking at one team that way, I told Sailor, "That's going to be us."

"Not yet."

"But it's going to be."

"And I say not yet." He said that barely able to stand.

I kept fussing with Judy and Mawd, straightening their lines and adjusting their straps the way they liked them. They were such a finicky pair, but the harnesses were molded to their forms, and they knew their exact fit. That old brown leather had been soaked with their sweat until it was soggy. But they pulled with it perfectly together. They were so even and balanced that no one strap was worn more than another. In fact, except for the reds, no other team in the field was as well matched. Judy and Mawd were the same size and strength, and their timing together was identical. They were a twin-powered machine at work.

But the reds were bigger and stronger.

By the fifth round six teams were left, and the hooves had chewed up the ground, digging in. The teams now were purposely excited and frightened to give them that extra nervous strength. They were stampeded around the field until the drivers barely reined control. "Hiii!! Hiii!!" The mules were charging, with their eyes rolling, their mouths frothing, and their hides lathered white.

It was a job for some of the drivers to restrain their teams enough to be hitched after racing them. But once they were, they'd slam against that weight with all that extra juice released and churn the ground, digging in and straining until their eyes popped and their mouths lopped open and they were left lurching, burned out in their traces.

We didn't have to stampede Judy and Mawd. Sailor only had to trot them a little and let them know by the way he talked that the sled would be heavier, the way he did with timber, and then'd he'd flick the reins with that touch he had, and I'd call them, and they'd give what was needed.

The big reds didn't need exciting either, but the blue coats ran them anyway, they made such a tremendous show charging and pounding the field. Heavily. You could feel the earth vibrating when they passed.

After the sixth round, only three teams were left. And after the seventh, only two. The reds and us. And the contest continued.

The sled was now loaded with 3500 pounds, and I didn't think we'd make it much farther. Judy and Mawd were sweated and Sailor was visibly weaker. His face was looking pinched.

"You can sit out," I told him. "I'll drive."

He brushed that aside with his hand.

"We can't win," I said.

"We're not out yet." But he said that dully.

I'd given up hope. We were going to lose Judy and Mawd, and we were just punishing them, keeping on. They'd pull their hearts out and we'd break their spirits, and we'd be doing it for nothing. Their eyes were telling me the story.

I sat down with Sailor, and we both looked at the ground. "One more time," I said. "We can make it look like we try and let it go, get it over with."

He gave me a long look and his mouth curled. "You mean, just *pretend*."

His edge on that cut me down.

We pulled the seventh round, and Judy and Mawd had to strain hard. The reds didn't.

At the eighth round the sled was loaded with the record weight of 3800 pounds that had been pulled only once before. The reds pulled first with the blue coats shagging them, and very simply, they skimmed the ground with the sled like it was nothing.

In our turn Judy and Mawd bogged in the mushy earth and were halted after five feet, but in their second try they made the distance. Sailor, though, had slapped the reins carelessly instead of flicking them. He was holding on but losing his touch.

Then, at 4000 pounds, a new record, the reds again pulled the ten feet in their first try and, surprisingly, Judy and Mawd did too.

And this time I saw something about that big red team, for the first time, or maybe I only heard it, but it was something about the way their trace chains snapped taut. They snapped all right, but not exactly together at the same time. There was a snap difference. It was as if one half the red team had pulled a fraction slower than the other.

Sailor noticed too, and it was a tiny thing, but I felt a new pulse in my chest.

When I glanced at the crowd, though, I knew they had no doubts. You could tell the way their eyes looked, the way their admiration was focused on the reds. They knew that team was just too overpowering, too much. Anything against that great pair, in their eyes, was hopeless. I saw Chubb smiling kindly, and I didn't look, but I imagined the Cranes' expressions. Still, the little pulse in my chest kept beating.

In the next round the reds came out the same, thundering, and then they were set for the hitch and lined up. It was going to be a repeat performance. They were going to display their same royalty and superiority again.

Then, for no reason, on the first try, the one on the left balked. The big mule simply planted its hooves and sat back. But only once. The driver got them lined up again and they made the distance in two more efforts.

I didn't think they were pulling well together now, but the ground was bad in that spot and I couldn't be sure.

Judy and Mawd also made it in only two tries, but it was two hard tries that took its toll and left their flanks quivering. They'd looked good with timing, with their bodies slanted exactly the same and their twin necks reaching, but the weight was getting overwhelming for any animals their size. At this point too, Sailor was fading fast. He was stumbling and catching himself against the sled.

But the contest went on.

With the weight at 4600 pounds, the reds came out lathered and blowing, and for once showed some tiredness and strain, but they still pulled the sled in two tries and made it look easy enough. They were so big, so damned colossal, they were making up in size for what they missed in timing.

It took us all three tries to make the distance, with Judy and Mawd giving it all they had, and with Sailor reeling on his feet.

But the crowd was caught up now in a different mood. I could sense it. And I could feel a part of the people pulling for us. They knew they were seeing something now. The reds weren't going to just walk away with it. They were in a fight to the finish, and we were giving it to them. The little guys were giving the big guys a run for their money and making them earn it. And we were nobody. We'd come from out of the trees, from nowhere, but we were sticking and we were giving the giants a battle. I could feel a hum in my bones now, the juices in me pumping new life. Maybe we can do it, I thought, maybe it's possible. I was suddenly alive with new hope.

But it was going to be close. Judy and Mawd were almost winded. Their eyes were shimmering with fatigue, and their endurance was hurt. They knew we were asking too much, and I put my arm around their soppy necks and hugged them. "Once more," I whispered, "once more, please."

And not the river rats. That flashed in me. Dammit, not the river rats!

The sled was being loaded again, and Sailor was sitting on the bench with his head hanging, his jaw slack.

I touched his shoulder. "You gonna make it?"

He mumbled.

"Sailor, we got to."

"I know."

"One more time."

"Yeh." He nodded slowly. But he wasn't exactly present.

The weight was 4800 pounds, a high mountain of weight on the sled. It would be like moving a mountain.

The reds came onto the field with their plumes flying and their trace chains jingling and their polished hooves pounding. They were tired now too, and their coats were sweated the color of dark blood, and they were slathering at the mouth, but the blue coat drove them hard around the field and they were still a great and dashing pair.

They heaved against the sled and started to pull, lost their balance, struggled it back, and then plowed up the ground in chunks. Before they were stopped, they had stretched the string tight its full length.

On their second try they threw their huge chests into the lunge and jerked the peg as they went to their knees. But the peg was just barely jerked, and when the reds were unhitched and led away, their sides were heaving and their eyes were glazed.

I rushed out to stamp the soft ground in front of the sled, to tromp it down as hard as I could, and then I went around Judy and Mawd, straightening their lines and straps. "We're gonna do it," I told them, and I gave their legs a fast rub.

It was our turn now.

Sailor trotted our pair around the field. I don't know how he kept up, but he did, and I ran alongside.

When we got around, Judy and Mawd both were breathing harder, but keyed up, and they backed to the sled with their skins jittering. I made the hitch and got back in front to align them. "It's okay," I told them, "it's okay."

Then Sailor flicked the reins and I called and they came. They plunged toward me, stabbing the ground, and the mountain behind came with them, a few feet, several feet, and then the weight held them.

We got them back and straight again, and I called them. "Come! C'mon, c'mon, Judymawd, Judymawd!" They reached for me again with their faces, found new ground with their hooves, and the sled was moving and coming with them, sliding, another foot, and another. They were straining through the leather, through their collars, and then they seemed to bunch and make a final lunge, all they could do, and the peg was sprung from its spot and popped high in the air.

The crowd was silent for a moment. I think, shocked. The peg had shot into the air. Then the applause came, and loud cheers. Judy and Mawd had just pulled 1000 pounds more than any other team their size.

But we still hadn't won. The sled was being loaded again, this time to 5000 pounds, and the reds again were coming out.

As we led Judy and Mawd from the field, their legs were trembling and they were faltering, trying to walk.

Sailor lay down on the bench and put his arms across his eyes. His face had turned livid on the last pull, but he had managed to finish. I stepped close to hear his breathing, and it sounded shallow.

"Sailor—"

His left foot off the bench twitched.

I nudged him carefully. "Sailor—"

"Go on." His voice was strong. "Lemme rest."

I turned back to the field.

The big reds were being whipped and stampeded around the arena to rev them to their highest pitch. They were flying in their shining harnesses, streaming sweat, and their mouths were open wide. Their hooves were pounding the ground and leaving clods hopping behind them.

They could hardly be contained for the hitch. Then they leaped forward, lunging with their great bodies, and the sled was moved—but not straight forward. It was skidded. One of the reds had lunged with less, and the sled had cornered and stopped, a few inches only in distance.

The driver reined them back, and they were aligned for a second try. You could tell they had good strength left, the way they moved. They could pull that weight if they wanted to, if they pulled together.

And this time, when they lunged again, they dragged the sled the distance except for a few inches. At the end they'd lost their balance and fishtailed. Their momentum was checked then and they were stopped. The line had paid out its length behind them, but it was slack yet, and the peg was still in place.

They needed only a little now to pluck the peg, a few inches, no more, but it was their last try coming, and I felt a tingle in my scalp.

The blue coats took their time. They limbered the chains and adjusted their lines. All that chrome was seated and patted down. Then the reds were carefully aligned to the load, straight as an arrow, and you had to believe they'd do it. They were getting bunched and ready.

The driver squared his feet, wrapped the reins around his hands, and took a breath. The final effort.

Then he slapped the reins. "Hawww!!"

And the reds lunged.

But not together, not exactly. They hit the weight a fraction off and their force was spread, their power was split, and with their thrust widened, they started pulling against each other. The driver was whipping them and yelling, but it was no good. The reds backed off the weight.

And that was it.

The sled remained in place with the string still slack and the peg still stuck.

Again the crowd was silent, but with a pall.

The reds were led from the field with their plumes broken where the driver had whipped them, and they somehow looked smaller. They had been spectacular, and they'd pulled a lot, but finally not together, and now their ears were drooped and their heads were hanging.

Chubb's face in the crowd was a blank. At the end of the field, the Cranes were standing, scowling.

I ran out and started stamping the loose dirt again. It was too soft in front of the sled, and I wanted to get it hard. Judy and Mawd had pulled all they could and I knew it, but I couldn't help myself. My heart was pounding, and we had one more chance—that's all I knew.

I hurried around Judy and Mawd, rubbing their legs. Sailor struggled to his feet and was trying to help, but I don't think he knew why. He'd lain with his arms across his eyes, and he hadn't seen the reds fail. He was simply following me.

Then it was time to move out.

Sailor took the reins and stared at them. And that's all he was doing, standing there staring at the reins in his hands.

I shook his arm. "Sailor, we gotta do it, we gotta do it!"

He repeated, "Yeah, we gotta do it."

He seemed to take hold.

As we went onto the field, I walked beside Judy and Mawd and patted their backs. It was no longer happening *out there*. It was close on now. And the only thing left was that weight on the sled sitting by itself in the middle of the field. A mountain to be moved, and nothing else was around.

Judy and Mawd backed automatically and I hitched them, adjusted their straps, limbered the chains, and took my place in front. Sailor fumbled the reins, clutched them up again, took his stance, and gave me the sign. I lined the team straight and gave their hot noses one last feel.

We were ready.

Sailor flicked the reins, and I called, "Come!"

Judy and Mawd lunged and hit hard against the weight. They had heart and they tried, but the sled didn't budge, not an inch. It was dead set with its runners pressed down in the dirt.

Judy's and Mawd's eyes were watery, pained. They'd hit a solid barrier they couldn't see, and they were hurting.

And just the same, we were going again.

But this time Sailor was lifting the reins stupidly. His touch was gone and he was going to slap the lines high and start the team wrong. He was playing his cards, smiling in general and looking and not seeing. He had that expression on his face. Someone had raised, and he was going to raise back, and he didn't care if he lost. It was the playing and that's all, not the game or the winning or losing. That's the look he had.

"Wait!" I ran back and grabbed the reins. He tried to hold them, but his hands were weak and let go.

I pushed him aside and stepped in his place.

I think he saw he was out of it then. "Okay," he

said. He wobbled and kept his feet. "Okay," he said, "you do it."

I pulled Judy and Mawd back in line and rubbed them. "All right, all right, it's all right now, easy," I said.

They knew it wasn't all right, but they held their places and tried to stand firm on trembling legs. Spasms showed signs in their withers.

"Easy, easy, it's all right." I pulled them back gently until they were exactly even and there was slack all the way in their traces. I let them know I had a good feel on the reins and that I was going to turn them loose with it. I was going to ask them for everything again and they were going to have to give it.

And because they knew I was asking, they'd give, they'd try. I could feel them sucking in, getting ready, arching their necks, pulling their chests up, rising to it. They were gathering all they could and shifting it back on their haunches.

When I sensed it was there and triggered back as far as it would go, I gave the reins a flick and let them have it. "Hoooo!!"

They came off their sets hurtling and hit against the weight perfectly on point and exactly, solidly together. It was a beautiful feeling, and they kept charging. Without any real strength, they had it going, they were so smooth. The sled became untracked and started moving. It didn't lurch free but eased out and started gliding, slowly.

The big mountain was slowly moving forward, and I kept urging, "That's it, that's it, that's it."

Their hooves kept digging steadily. Their slender legs were stabbing like pistons. They were slanting low to the ground and pulling with their hearts. The string began to pay out behind the sled. They were straining beyond their limit, but still they pulled, and the string began to show its length.

The veins in their necks were swollen to bursting, but their heads kept reaching and their bodies kept plunging until the line was straight and lifting from the ground.

And then it was too much. Their legs went out from under them, and they were stumbling, and that was it.

I looked back. The string was stretched taut from sled to peg. I could see the tension in it, and all we needed was a fraction more to jerk the peg, a sliver more, a kiss, that's all—we'd come so close.

But Judy and Mawd were down, hanging in their straps, their legs crumpled under them. They'd been pushed too far, they'd given too much, and even their own weight was too much for them now. Their sides were heaving.

I felt suddenly weak and physically beaten. I couldn't move. Then—

A hand touched me.

Sailor was beside me. His face was gray, and he was swaying, but his eyes were hard. They were burning, and he was taking the reins from my hands. "Not yet," he said. "Not yet."

He was his own purpose and moving past me to Judy and Mawd.

"We can't," I said.

But he was already whipping their heads with the reins and kicking their legs. He was forcing them up, and they were struggling to their feet, their eyes wild and rolling white. He kept slapping their faces until they were hobbling back in their traces, and he whipped them harder to go back on their haunches. Then he stepped behind and lashed out and cut them.

They lunged forward and smashed against the weight, and again they fell, crashed to their bellies, and the sled didn't move.

But it was jarred. It was shocked, and a tremor passed through it. The taut string caught the tremor and vibrated and the peg at the end of the string was shivering. It was rising from the earth, and it was happening in an instant, in a wink, but I watched that peg rising for an eternity. While the clouds rose and the vacuum pulled my face. The grains of sand around the peg were falling away, and I watched. While a calmness descended and stillness spread itself in the air. The peg was upright and holding to its point.

Then I saw the tension in the string relaxed and loosened. The peg had toppled onto its side out of the hole.

It appeared such a slight thing, lying there, without content, without meaning—

Sailor dropped the reins and staggered away.

People were coming down from the stands.

·   ·   ·

Spoon Crane was trying to stomp the peg back in the ground. He'd run up, waving his arms and yelling, "It ain't jerked! Look, it ain't jerked! They cheated!"

Maybe a splinter from his broken nose had finally pierced his brain, he'd suddenly gone so berserk. He was raving and stomping on the peg like some kind of lunatic. The crowd around was giving him room, and even Collard and Ham were standing back with an amazed look on their dull faces.

But they were in back of the sled, and I didn't care.

I was seeing about Judy and Mawd.

They were still down in front of the sled in a tangle of harnesses, their heads flat to the ground, their mouths caked with foam and dirt. A thin fluid was leaking from their noses, and their legs were twitching. I was feeling for damage. Their hides were soaked like spongy carpets, but their limbs were sound, their hooves were whole, and they were breathing well enough. Some muscles were probably strained, some tendons, maybe blood vessels were burst, but I could tell they were going to make it.

The worst thing, though, was their eyes. They'd always been trusting, but when I pulled to free their straps, they weren't. They looked at me fearfully.

Then Spoon jumped me from the back, and it felt like a dog attacking. He was snarling and biting, and he had me pinned with his body. He had my ear in his teeth, and I could feel his jaw grinding. I could smell his rancid mouth.

Several men stepped in to pull him off, and they were grappling with him, but he was clawing and sticking. Then someone slammed him in the nose and his mouth broke open with a howl and his head was yanked away.

They held him kicking and struggling, an arm locked around his throat, and he was still snarling, "I'll gitcha! I'll gitcha!" The dirty tape was hanging by a corner, blood was pouring from his smashed nose, and his eyes were insane.

The arm around his neck jerked him off his feet and dragged him away, strangling and kicking.

I wiped at my ear with my shirttail and Spoon's grinding jaw was still sounding in my head. "Your ear's all right," someone said. But he's not finished, I thought. My shirttail was coming away bloody and slimy with his saliva. The pull's settled, Hominy's leaving, but he's gonna keep on. And I better find Sailor, I thought. He'd disappeared.

He could bring his mind back before his body was ready, when he was out of it. And I knew he could do that. I'd seen him raise his wrecked body too many times. But maybe this time was the last. He'd brought himself back to make the final pull, but maybe this time he'd used himself up entirely. He wasn't there when Spoon jumped me, and he wasn't there to see about Judy and Mawd.

I finally found him behind the bleachers lying on his back. I thought he was dead, but he'd only passed out. Or he had passed out and remained resting. When I touched him, he moved. "Hey, Sailor," I said, and he opened his eyes. Yellowish sick eyes.

Then he grinned. "We won, didn't we?"

I plopped down beside him. "Yeah—we won."

He managed to sit up. "Judy and Mawd?"

"They're still down. I think we broke 'em."

"Their spirits?"

"Yeh. I think we did. The last time." Everything in me seemed to drain into the ground.

"Maybe not," he said. But we didn't go on with it.

We let the air settle. And I looked off.

The field had been left a torn-up battleground. All the troops had been killed off. Only a couple of bodies were left twitching. It had taken too much.

"Your ear," Sailor said, "looks like somebody chewed on it."

"I 'magine it does," I said, and we didn't go on with that either.

After a while Sailor stood up and tested his balance. And in another minute, when we started walking, he appeared to have his strength back. It had appeared for some time to ebb and flow in him. Like a tide. But the flow each time seemed to be a little further out.

I thought I glimpsed Hominy and Darryl in the crowd once, in the distance. He had his hat cocked on the back of his head, and he was trying to walk with his arm around her waist but she was pulling away—I could've told him. You don't keep trying to hold. You let her go. And what might have been, or should have been, you let that go too.

Chubb paid off without grumbling. He simply tallied our bets and handed over the cash.

"Them mules," he said, "they showed a lotta heart, didn't they?"

I got my fifty bucks, plus another hundred and fifty. Sailor's take was over a thousand with his hundred at three-to-one odds, the Cranes' five hundred, and the several bets he'd made on the side, which Chubb also had held.

"You still want a job," Chubb told me, "you got it. You can start Monday." He squeezed my shoulder. "Yessir, you handled yourself all right out there."

He chuckled and shook his head.

Judy and Mawd got on their feet finally and we led them back to their pasture.

I thought they walked differently, listlessly more than just weakly, but they held themselves well enough, and we staked them in a good patch of grass.

"A couple more days," Sailor said, "they'll come back around."

"They might not be the same, though." I was noticing the lower way they held their ears. "They might not have the heart again for the heaviest timber."

"Well, we'll just have to wait and see."

Their slender hooves had once stepped so sprightly, their high haunches had once rolled so gracefully. What I saw now made me turn away with an ache in my throat. They'd started moving like robots and they were grazing without interest, mechanically.

We ain't gonna be *mechanized*, Sailor had always said, but now we were.

I checked to see that my things were still in the wagon, and again I left them.

.   .   .

In my room, Sailor was in bed and I was sitting in the chair against the wall. He'd gotten sicker, trying to eat at the café.

"You don't have to stay," he said.

But what would I do now, on my own? Where would I go now, alone? "I don't mind," I said.

"You can go on," he said. "I don't need a nurse."

"I can sit. I'm not bothering you."

"Yeh, you are. You're sitting there like the kiss of death."

"You don't have to look."

"I thought you wanted to get away."

"Maybe I changed my mind."

He regarded me solemnly. "Ya know, you could do that," he said. "You could stick around, give it another year maybe. It wouldn't hurt."

"I might."

"I never said I wanted you to leave." He tried to smile.

"That's right," I said, "you never did."

He closed his eyes then, and his body seemed to sink under the covers. His forehead was damp. His face looked hot, and for the first time I noticed the gray in his whiskers.

"You oughta see a doctor," I said.

"When I get to feeling bad enough, I will." He spoke without opening his eyes. And it was the same old story. He was going to get well on his own, and if he didn't, he was going to walk through that last door the same way he'd walked through every door his whole life.

He went to sleep, breathing regularly.

The last door. But not that night.

He'd rise again to swing an ax, and I'd never see his actual death, but when I think of Sailor dying, I think of that night, sitting in that chair, watching him breathe.

The breath of life was still in him. And watching, I thought, the breath of life—so simple. But said that way, that's a single breath, and life is more than that. It's breathing regularly past the moment, on and on, and Sailor was doing that.

And I was watching.

Just remember, kid, there ain't no wealth but life.

No wealth at all beyond the door.

We'd searched and found nothing. No, something. We found what was out there. Which was nothing. Which we

*wouldn't have found if we hadn't looked, so that makes it
something.*

A knock on the door. The last door, I felt. But it
was only Lew tapping, and he was whispering, "Bud?"

I glanced at Sailor still sleeping, and opened the
door quietly.

Lew's face was anxious. "There's someone here to
see you," he whispered. "A girl. She says you know
her."

A figure down the hall at the entrance. The back
was turned, one hip cocked.

"I don't allow girls—" Lew was saying, but I was
already walking past him.

"I only got a minute," Hominy said. "Darryl's waiting."

She was almost in shadow in the dim entrance,
but her lips were bright red and her eyes were shining.
I felt again her special presence and that strange close-
but-not-touching feeling between us.

"I'm leaving tonight," she said. "A storm's coming,
and Darryl wants to go on."

"Now?"

"Yeh, it's supposed to flood and get bad."

I couldn't quite talk. She'd come to see me purposely, and she was so pretty.

"I think we got a spy." Hominy gestured behind
us, and when I looked, Lew ducked back into his office.

"That's just Lew," I said. "He's all right."

"He didn't act very friendly."

"I don't think he allows girls."

"He can look, I don't care." She lowered her eyes.
"You walked away last night, I didn't feel right. I
shoulda told you good-bye too."

"I didn't give you much of a chance."

"I probably won't see you again." Our eyes met and she immediately looked away. "Maybe you'll think about me sometime."

"I will—I'll think about you a lot."

"You know what?" She tried to smile. "You taught me something. Double negatives. I needed to know that."

A horn sounded outside.

She shrugged. "Darryl."

I couldn't look at her. "I hope Dallas turns out for you."

"It will. A big place like that, they're gonna have lots of jobs, lots of places I can get on." She was trying to sound casual, but I saw her mouth tighten.

"And what about money?"

"I'll get by."

"Just the same—" I pulled the folded money from my pocket and put it in her hand. "You're gonna need this."

Her mouth opened, but no words.

"It's two hundred dollars. You can have it."

She appeared stung, and she stared at the money. "Two hundred—"

"I don't need it. I won it."

"But I'll have to owe you."

"It's okay." She looked soft in the dim light.

The horn sounded again, twice.

"I just came to say good-bye." Her mouth was twisting. "You're just nice, ain'tcha?"

"Not nice—"

"Yeh, you are, all the time." Her eyes were suddenly brimming and she tried to wipe them, but the money in her hand got in the way.

I felt embarrassed.

"I didn't ask for this," she said.

"I know."

"You didn't have to do this." Her voice was choked.

Her tears were streaming her cheeks faster than she could wipe them and she turned to hide her face. "Look what you got me doing," she said, but not sobbing.

I almost reached to hold her, but pulled back. Her shoulders were shaking and her face was in her hands. But she was not exactly crying, not with sounds.

The horn now was one long obnoxious blaring.

"Sounds like he wants to go," I said.

She finally straightened and wiped her face and spoke to the horn. "Oh, shut up!"

The horn abruptly stopped as if commanded.

"He must've heard," I said.

"He just can't wait." She was still turned and not facing me.

"Well, if a storm's coming—"

"Yeh, we better go." She was looking down at the money in her hand, smoothing the bills absently. "I'm sorry I said I didn't like you. I didn't mean it."

"It's okay. I didn't get mad."

"I wish things were different."

"Maybe they will be. When you get to Dallas."

"I just want to forget."

"Maybe you can." I felt awkward, waiting behind her.

Then she turned and I wished she hadn't. Her eyes were red and her face was unnaturally strained. It was so full of pain, it seemed, so ugly in pain.

"I'm never gonna forget you," she said. "I mean it, I never will."

She moved quickly and gave me a fast peck on the lips and ran out the door.

I heard a car door slam, a motor roar, and screeching tires pulling away. She'd been holding the money tight, and I was seeing that, the squeezed grasp she had.

Then, "Who was that?"

Lew had sneaked up behind me and I turned on him. "Dammit, Lew, don't do that!"

He blinked. "She was crying."

"No, she wasn't."

"I saw her—"

"I don't care, she wasn't crying." I stomped past him.

Sailor was still sleeping and I was sitting in the chair again in the dark room.

She's gone, I thought, and that's it.

But what was it? There was a rumble of thunder somewhere, and I was dimly aware the storm was coming. They had wanted to get out ahead of it and they were driving away now and she was sitting beside him, the pale glow of the dash lights on her face. A tight fist in her lap, inside her, dead to the music. Holding. On her bed beside me she had slumped and looked like a doll tossed aside without regard. But mostly she was holding. And working to continue. In a big place like Dallas you could find yourself a job and go on, one step at a time. You could get lost in the crowd, and nobody would know you. A big place like that, you could be anybody and never be found. I never knew when the rain began. It was simply there. Falling. But she needed to go, and she'd keep going. I go with somebody, she said, that doesn't make 'em a boyfriend. Or anything. A seed was buried, but it had a little shoot pushing to break through the crust. Maybe it would. She was tough. I'm remembering. You don't even have a car, she said. At least he had a car. A get-away car with screeching tires. Escaping in the night. The glow of the dash lights on her face, a fist closed tight in her lap, in her heart, and there I was, I keep remembering.

.   .   .

When the storm broke, Sailor rose.

"Judy and Mawd," he said. "C'mon."

I'd been dozing in the chair, but I woke instantly with the fear that something bad was happening.

"We can take 'em to the fair grounds," he said, "get 'em under shelter." He was striding down the hall as if in a storm at sea again. He had his sea legs back, and he was on a windswept deck.

I felt we were going into danger, bucking the waves. And it was almost like that. The rain was pouring in heavy sheets and rushing the street. The sky was thundering, and we had to lean into the wind. The lightning was cracking in jagged limbs.

But we pushed through. We hurried.

Then, near the pasture, we heard the sound of a motor, a sputtering sound going away. It was instantly familiar and unmistakable, and I knew we were too late. I saw the red blink of a taillight through the trees and in my mind I saw the old pickup truck with chicken wire and Spoon's leering face. Tire tracks seeping mud curved from the pasture and followed the fading sputter.

We were too late, I knew, and I ran ahead of Sailor into the pasture.

Lightning illuminated my ax from the wagon. It had been tossed aside in the field and the blade was reflecting a glistening sheen.

Beyond, Judy and Mawd were on the ground in the rain. In flashes, I saw each had hooves missing, and they were thrashing the air with legs like stems.

Sailor was moving past me, picking up the ax, and he was walking toward them.

I couldn't look.

We were standing in the rain and the lightning was breaking around us. That's the picture I see and the weather absorbed everything. The wind was blowing and our clothes were plastered to our bodies, but there's no actual feel of the weather in my picture. And there's no feeling in me.

Sailor was still holding the ax in one hand down at his side and his face was bleak and streaming. His eyes were dark holes.

"I had to," he said.

Barely heard, a sound in the distance, in the first line of trees. A starter faintly buzzing, whirring. A drowned motor trying to start. There's a sputter and the starter is whirring again, a sound so thin it could be imagined, but the wind is carrying it.

"You go on back," he said.

"You come with me."

"Find the police. Tell 'em what happened, what they did."

"What about you?"

"Never mind, go on." His lips were tight. His hair was flat and strangely parted by the rain.

"I better come with you," I said. "There's three of 'em."

"No, you go on. Do what I say."

I felt sick. It was all ending and I didn't want to be alone. "Sailor, please—" My words faded.

"You just find the police, tell 'em what they did to Judy and Mawd." His grip on the ax handle had tightened.

"Sailor—"

"Bud—" He gave me that look. It was settled. But he also spoke softly and touched my shoulder gently. "This is my business now, and I want you outta here. Go on."

I had no mind. I only knew it was ending and that's the way it was. His touch on my shoulder lingered, and then it was pushing me.

As I turned, a flash revealed the two dark lumps in the watery field, cold and still, a rushing stream banking against them.

The distant starter was slowing and turning by halves. The battery behind it was running down, sucking out of juice. And the rain was blinding.

The storm would last the night. It would cause the flood. The roads were going to be washed out, people were going to drown, and the town would sink knee-deep in water before it was over, but I didn't know that then. I only knew I was out in it and going through it.

When I found the police, they were pulling a marooned car from an underpass and setting up roadblocks. They were bogging in mud, and the wind and rain were whipping their slickers.

"Look, we got our hands full," one said. "We'll get to you when we can."

They had set out flares, spewing fiery sticks, and the red light on their car kept flashing their faces.

"You got mules," one said. "Hell, we got people out in this getting their damn-fool selves drowned. That river's coming outta its banks, can't you see nothing?"

Then, "Where'd you say? Hell, that place's gone by now. You can't even get back there. Look at that water."

So they didn't come. They couldn't.

And I almost didn't get back. The water had risen above my knees in some places, and once a rolling wave in a sudden torrent knocked me down, but I made it.

Or almost.

Because the place really was gone. I saw from a mound of high ground. What had been the flat pasture was a wide surging river, and a strong current was creasing it with seams. It showed in the whitening glow that came and went in the sky and resounded with thunder. There was no crossing it to the trees, and they were flooded too.

There was no sign of what had been Judy and Mawd, and the wagon was gone, all underwater or swept away. And there was no sign of Sailor. The place where he'd stood was a swirling eddy.

The storm, the pouring rain and wind, and the roaring of the flood were over all.

There was nothing I could do but stand, and I don't know how long I lasted. I saw whole trees tumbling by with their torn roots thrashing in the waves. I saw the river rushing to sweep the hills.

He'd been gripping the ax tighter. His eyes had been dark holes. But his touch had lingered. He'd let me know.

Sailor! Dammit! Come back! Sailor, dammit, I'm calling you!

But he was gone. He was nowhere. And a chill was in me, deep down.

. . .

I was sick in my room for three days with a fever, the first time ever, and Lew took care of me. A doctor came by and gave me medicine and told me to rest.

I don't recall a lot that I felt or thought. I suppose I had dreams, and I have the impression parts of my life passed before me, but nothing important. I remember feeling glad Hominy had gotten away, that she was better off in a new place, but I couldn't imagine her in Dallas. I saw her instead walking along, carrying a suitcase. And I remember a certain feeling for Sailor's absence, the fact that he was absent, but nothing more.

Lew was always fussing over me, putting wet towels on my forehead and trying to feed me soup. Every time I opened my eyes, I saw his worried face and little white hands. I kept telling him to get away and leave me alone, and he'd look hurt and back off, but never for long. I suppose I should have been grateful. When I finally ate the soup, it wasn't that bad.

The third day I was still in bed but getting well, and Lew brought me the newspaper.

Front page. Five people had drowned in the flood. Two were an older couple caught in a gully. The other three were the Cranes.

Collard and Ham were found in their pickup submerged in the flood, and they were definitely drowning victims, the paper said. But Spoon's story was a little different. His body was found washed up in a pile of driftwood, and he could have died in an accident first, the paper said. His skull was split and his face was badly battered, but since he was also caught in the flood, the force could have dashed his head against the rocks as it swept him along. So his death was chalked up to that.

There was no mention of Sailor, but in my heart I knew he was dead too. I could see his tattoos bleaching in the sun.

"Sailor?" Lew asked.

"I don't know," I said.

"I could report him missing—?"

I waved him away. "Just leave me alone, will ya?"

.   .   .

Sailor is stalking. He's moving like a ghost through the trees and the Cranes are pushing their pickup. It's sticking in mud but hard ground allows them to push it faster and it's starting. Sailor is hurrying, and the pickup is chugging to life. Collard is behind the wheel and Ham is jumping in but Spoon is still pushing at the door. His head is a target and the ax is spinning through the rain like a shiny propeller. Lightning strikes and water is rising in the trees. The flood is rushing in and the pickup is swept away. Spoon's body is lifted in a foaming tide and tumbling. Sailor is standing out in it, raising his arms to it, and he's calling it down. "You're crazy," I yell. "You're gonna get struck!" But he doesn't care. He's laughing. Then his face is down in mine. "Hey, kid, whatcha scared of?" Suddenly the air explodes in our faces, and when I look again, loose lines are dangling in the trees. There's a blank spot where Judy and Mawd should have been and the sound of their hooves is splashing away in the storm. Then we're floating in the

*shallows, and it's calm. The river is safe. "Now ain't you
ashamed?" Sailor says.*

.   .   .

I was getting well, and the room without windows was
depressing me. I needed to be outside, to breathe in the
open air again, and I needed to be gone.

I was dressed and leaving.

"I reported him missing," Lew said.

"He's not missing."

"Well, he hasn't showed up. He could be lost."

"Not that either."

"Anyway, I reported him missing. I thought we
should."

"And what'd the police say?"

"They said they'd keep an eye out. I gave them his
description."

I looked at him. "What description?"

Lew blinked. "Well, you know, big and dark, sort
of mean-looking—"

"Mean-looking?"

"Well, yes, sort of."

"Sailor wasn't mean."

"No, not mean." Lew was nervous that he'd said
the wrong thing. "But maybe sort of rough-looking."

"That's closer." I started out.

Lew, as usual, pursued. "You're coming back?"

"I told you, I'm going to work, at the sawmill."

"But you're not well yet."

"I'm well enough."

"You should rest another day—"

"Lew, dammit, cut that out!" That stopped him.

At the door I turned again. "Rough-looking's all
right," I said. "But if he shaved and dressed up, he
might not've looked that way either."

As I left, Lew was holding his hands and trying to smile. And that's the last time I saw him.

He probably knew I wasn't going to work at the sawmill, that I'd only told him that. But if I said good-bye, I was afraid he'd cry on me—and he probably knew that too.

The same as before, Pauline was in bed with her head propped on pillows, and she was squinting from being awakened. I knew Sailor wouldn't be there, I knew where he was, but she might have seen him one last time, and if she had, I wanted to know that.

"I just thought he might've come by," I said, "to get out of the storm."

"Don't think so," she said. "Not since the storm. Business has been pretty slow." A slice of her round thigh was showing at the edge of the covers.

"Well, he was sick—"

"And I'm supposed to run a hospital?" She yawned. "I told you, honey, I run a cathouse. Somebody gets sick and wants to die, they can go someplace else."

"I was just checking."

"If I see him, I'll tell him you asked. Now, go on, I need my sleep." She fluffed at her pillow.

Her thigh was only fat to me now. Her orangy hair was ugly. "I'm sorry I bothered you," I said.

"Yeah, well, you come back when you got some money to spend." She yawned again. "And when you're a little older. I'll be awake then." She closed her eyes.

For ten, you get a quickie, and they get you in and out as fast as they can. For fifty, you get all night and a little more conversation. But for fifty, you might as well talk to yourself.

"I'm leaving," I said, but I don't think she heard

me. I wanted to say, "You could've acted a little more interested too." But I didn't bother.

Behind me, when I got to the stairs, I heard her snoring.

Rita was in the hall when I came down and she looked at me without recognition. She was in her ratty robe and woolly socks, and I thought again how she needed a longer robe to cover her knees, they were such knobby-looking things.

Old Stella opened the door for me with her crippled hands. She never smiled and I wondered again if she ever did. When she was young and pretty, did she ever have fun? Poor old woman, I thought. And I walked through the door.

.   .   .

Drift was piled high in some places, in the branches of trees, and there were fences down and new ravines in the ground, but the flood had receded and my going back to camp was easy enough.

As I walked into the clearing, the place looked the same. The flood hadn't touched it. But there was a different feel in the air somehow. The tent, the fire pod, the food box, the tools—all the same. But they also appeared too fixed, too still, and it was strange. It was the feel of nobody home, and it took me a moment.

Then I spotted him. I might have missed him at first glance, but he was there and I knew he would be.

He was sitting at the side of the clearing with his back to a tree and he was staring down at his hands. I thought he looked the same. Then I walked over and he looked like somebody who could have passed for his twin. But not quite. The ears maybe, I couldn't tell exactly. The ears looked too big to be Sailor's, and the neck was too thin. And his nose appeared too long. And his head too bony. Suddenly it seemed it didn't look like anybody I'd ever known, and I felt irritated, as if I'd made a mistake. What had appeared to be Sailor, what could have been him, wasn't him at all.

Sailor was gone and nowhere around.

I had imagined him dead, but this was different. This was real.

He'd left his money in his keep-safe box buried beneath his bedroll and he'd written a note to go with it:

> *Bud, this is for you —*
> *not much but maybe — you*
> *can use it —*
> *~~just remember~~ S.*

I could see him starting the last sentence, some piece of advice, some thought or whatever, and then, feeling too weak, he'd decided against it and crossed it out. His hand was shaky, and I never listened, so why bother?

I sat with the note a long time without moving.

I felt his hand on my shoulder and his eyes looking at me. He'd never called me son, and I'd never called him dad, and now it was too late. The camp was empty, the trees were deserted, and the rest was beyond me, out of reach. A loneliness filled me, and I wasn't ready to be alone. I wasn't ready to go on my own.

And I wasn't leaving, I told you, I changed my mind and you said I could do that, you said I could give it another year and it wouldn't hurt— Dammit, Sailor, you come back, I'm calling you!

Sailor and me. Judy and Mawd. We'd lived together as a family. We'd worked as partners. I'd had my place. And now I didn't.

I suppose I sat there a little crazy, a little scared.

But you take steps and you keep going, she said, you keep going till you make it all the way. But all the way where? Till you live like you want, I said.

Till you live like you want, and even if you couldn't, you take steps and keep going. That's what you do.

Get up and c'mon, I said, get up and get started.

. . .

I'd like to say I buried Sailor in the trees where I found him, where he belonged, but there were too many roots.

I dug his grave in the clearing, and because he was rigid in his sitting position, the hole was more square than otherwise. I wrapped him in the tent, tied the bundle with a rope, and rolled it down into the hole. Then I laid his ax on top, layered rocks, and covered the rocks with topsoil which was rich and moist, and I patted it smooth. Maybe a tree would sprout in that spot and reach down to him. Maybe he could become a tree.

I didn't say any last words.

And I didn't stick around. Somebody else could have the job at the sawmill, and Lew could save my room or not, I didn't care. I didn't want anything reminding me.

I took Sailor's money, about a thousand dollars, and with his bedroll over my shoulder, I headed west.

He'd been to San Francisco, he said. He'd stood in the middle of Golden Gate Bridge and looked down. The moon was reflected on the water, he said, and it was a pretty sight.

Maybe I'd see it that way too. It was all just beyond those hills.

. . .

When Judy and Mawd appear now, I see them in their night places resting easy. Judy's on the right, and Mawd's left. They're standing asleep and dreaming, and sometimes I feel their dream is me.

Hominy, too, returns, and in my mind she's forever in the river, dipping down and coming up, streaming rivulets, her arms like splashing oars, splashing white. I see her glistening in the falling light, and to me, still, she's a shining sight.

And I still see Sailor with his ax. He stands wide, and his swing is long and powerful, graceful and easy. Every arch he cuts through the air is a perfect curve and his aim never misses. He slices through the wood so cleanly and smoothly there's no hurt, and the trees to him are like individuals. He likes to talk to them and touch at them. Then he goes on and chops them down. He never used a saw, he said, because there was no truth in that.

And I keep remembering, that's the way he talked. Trust yourself. There ain't no wealth but life. I keep hearing his voice around me, in the air, in the calmest places—

And the trees remain.